The Girl and the Witch's Garden

Praise for *The Girl and the Witch's Garden*

"As enchanting as it is wise, the true magic of this secret garden story is in its unflinching, heart-wrenching exploration of grief, belonging, and inner strength. Once I stepped into the witch's garden with Piper, I did not want to leave."
—Jessica Khoury, author of *The Mystwick School of Musicraft*

"Piper Peavey is a protagonist all her own in a spellbinding story that has a touch of *Miss Peregrine's Home for Peculiar Children* and a dab of *Circus Mirandus*."
—Quinn Sosna-Spear, author of *The Remarkable Inventions of Walter Mortinson*

"Magical and mysterious, a captivating read from start to beautiful end."
—Meg Frazer Blakemore, author of *The Water Castle* and *The Story Web*

"When Piper's father returns to the hospital to fight off another bout of cancer, Piper is sent to live with her grandmother and estranged mother at Mallory Estate. But the estate, her mother, the foster kids who live there, and the back garden ALL have secrets, and Piper is sucked into a mystery which is absolutely riveting. This book has strong *Secret Garden* vibes with a magical twist and a plot that races. Erin Bowman has penned a must read for middle graders!"
—Nichole Cousins, Still North Books & Bar (Hanover, New Hampshire)

"Erin Bowman has perfectly captured both the magic and loneliness of being a kid. A creepy house, a daring rescue, a magic portal, a secret garden—this book has everything that the best books of my childhood had. The characters are vibrant and real, and their problems take more than magic to solve—though the magic definitely helps!" —Megan Szmyd, Old Firehouse Books (Fort Collins, Colorado)

"A hugely entertaining new twist on magic! With gorgeously described fantastical elements, savvy kids, and some heartbreaking truths, Erin Bowman has woven a wonderful tale full to the brim with characters you'll want to follow far beyond the last page." —Alicia Michielli, Talking Leaves Books (Buffalo, New York)

"Bowman's new novel has everything you could want in a middle-grade book: magic, mystery, relatable characters, and a world you can get lost in. Piper will have readers imagining what their own affinities might be and longing for them to manifest, and the Mallory Estate is sure to inspire hidden-world fantasies. I loved getting lost in this story and can't wait to share it with fans of other kids' classics old and modern, from *The Secret Garden* to *Harriet the Spy* to *Three Times Lucky* and *Nevermoor*."
—Melissa Oates, Fiction Addiction (Greenville, South Carolina)

"A big, spooky house, a likable bunch of capable kids, and a refreshing (if bittersweet) acceptance of the face that there are some things not even magic can fix."
—*Bulletin of the Center for Children's Books*

The Girl and the Witch's Garden

ERIN BOWMAN

Simon & Schuster Books for Young Readers
New York London Toronto Sydney New Delhi

For my children

And for any child who has ever dreamed
of discovering a secret portal in their backyard

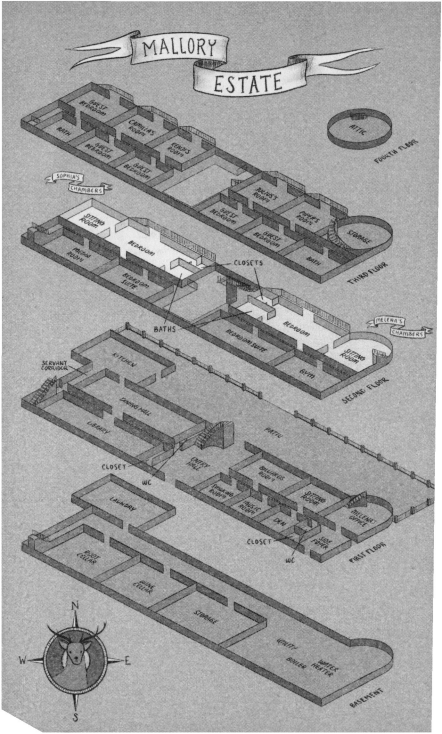

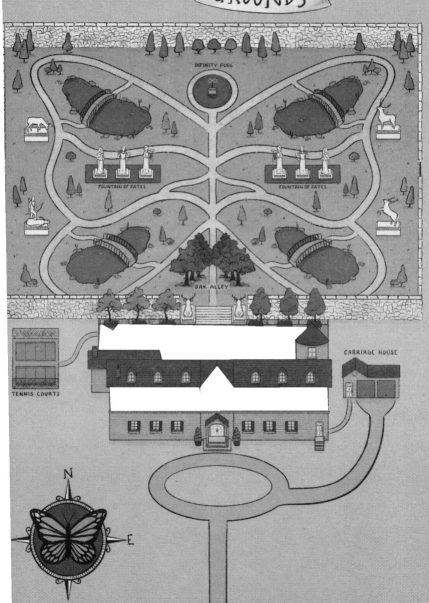

Chapter One

Welcome to Mallory Estate

There was no denying that a witch lived at Mallory Estate.

Grown-ups were fooled by the property's manicured front drive and the mansion's historic brick facade. *Regal*, they called it. *Charming*. But the problem with grown-ups is that they see what they want. They don't really look. Not properly, at least.

The children of Blackburn, however, knew the truth. They biked onto the grounds. They spied with binoculars. They rapped the door knocker and ran like they'd never run before. They discovered, through keen observation and a healthy dose of nosiness, what the grown-ups hadn't.

Things were not right at Mallory Estate.

For starters, it was always colder there. And damp. Even

when the sun was shining, it felt as though the grounds were perpetually shrouded in mist and fog and early-morning dew.

Second, the gardens out back were dead. The grass was brown and the flower beds brittle and the row of grand oak trees stood like skeletons, barren no matter the season.

When you looked closely at the house itself, past the details the adults admired, you could see that it was dying too. Paint had peeled off the window trim, and the roof needed repairing. Ivy was eating away at the bricks. It climbed the front wall, converging above the portico, then turned sharply, every last tendril growing toward *one* window. The highest window of the lone turret on the eastern side.

A figure sometimes lurked there, peering down at the grounds from behind a sheer curtain. Sometimes the witch was alone. Sometimes the cat was with her. It was a white cat, which always threw off the grown-ups. But the children knew.

Because if you made eye contact with the witch—if you looked for too long—she'd put a curse on you. She'd lure you up the front steps and compel you to raise the knocker.

And when it fell, and the front door was opened, then you were trapped.

The children knew the witch's secrets, and that was why she kept them. Once they entered Mallory Estate, they never came out.

○ ○ ○

Piper Peavey had grown up hearing stories about the witch of Mallory Estate.

Piper wasn't from Blackburn, but even two towns over, where she lived in a small bungalow with her father, Atticus, the stories were told. The tales had grown roots, much like the ivy on the estate, and spread through the sleepy towns of rural northwestern Connecticut, fascinating and terrifying schoolchildren in the same breath.

Piper, however, shrugged them off. She read enough fantasy books to know that things like witches and curses belonged in books, and that the real world was a very boring, sensible place. It was full of reason and rules and logical explanations. It lacked magic.

It was because of her practicality that Piper approached Mallory Estate with the same skepticism the grown-ups did, finding excuses for all the oddities.

The grounds, for example, were damp and cool because the estate was situated in a valley. The gardens were dead because a fire had destroyed them years earlier. And the house was beginning to deteriorate because that's what houses do when their owners fail to care for them. They slowly fall apart.

There was also the fact that the owner of the estate, Melena M. Mallory, was Piper's grandmother. And if Piper's grandmother were a witch, Piper would know it. She wasn't extremely close with the woman, but she saw her often enough to be sure.

Her grandma drove a pearl-white convertible—perhaps the least witchy mode of transportation imaginable—and she had a perfectly sensible job as an archivist; if she was familiar with cauldrons or potions, it was only through historic documents. She'd also attended every single one of Piper's childhood birthday parties, cheering as Piper blew out her candles with exactly the sort of enthusiasm you'd expect of a doting grandmother. When Piper turned ten and began having sleepovers with friends in lieu of afternoon parties, Grandma Mallory had started a tradition of taking Piper out to lunch the very next day. Wherever Piper liked. Friendly's that first year, then the Cheesecake Factory when she turned eleven and twelve.

Piper had even been to Mallory Estate herself. *Once.* It was the Christmas after her parents had divorced, when her father still believed that holiday dinners as a family might be possible. Sure, she'd been only five at the time, but she recalled the estate being a very big and boring residence, without a single trace of trapped children like the stories claimed. Plus, Piper had walked safely out of the house at the end of the evening, hand in hand with her father, which threw a wrench in the entire "once you go in, you're stuck there forever" theory.

No, nothing about Mallory Estate was very suspicious, and her grandmother was most certainly *not* a witch.

But, late in the afternoon on the first Monday of summer

vacation, as the car turned onto the estate's gravel drive, Piper felt a shiver run down her spine nonetheless. Maybe there was a *very* small piece of her that wanted her grandmother's house to be brimming with magic and curses and spells. Magic—even of the wicked variety—would be a wonderful distraction. More likely it was the fact that her father's latest round of chemo hadn't brought the results the doctors had hoped for, and the thought of spending the summer at Mallory Estate as he underwent even more radiation, alone, made Piper tremble.

The ghost of the shiver still lingered when the mansion appeared through the car's windshield. It was massive. Three stories tall (four if you counted the turret). Piper could see why adults used the word *regal* to describe it, but it was too intimidating to be charming.

"I don't understand why I can't stay with you," she groaned from the back seat.

"I told you already," Aunt Eva answered. "Client conflicts. I'll be in Colorado for most of the summer, starting work on that big account I landed last month."

Piper's aunt Evangeline was in marketing. She lived just a few miles from Piper and her father and worked from a quaint office in the Farmington Valley. Occasionally she had to travel to New York or Boston for a few days, but spending nearly all summer halfway across the country? Piper blew out a disgruntled breath.

It wasn't that she'd made grand plans for the summer. Piper hadn't been invited to Bridget Caldwater's pool party (and the entire town seemed to be invited); Piper was used to her classmates treating her like she was invisible, but she'd held out hope that her ex–best friend would stop ignoring her. No such luck. Even so, Piper would have preferred to be at the bungalow. She clutched her locket through her shirt, thinking of the packed bookshelf back home. It would have kept her plenty busy.

"You can come stay with me as soon as I'm back," her aunt continued, glancing at Piper in the rearview mirror. Her eyes were stormy gray, just like Piper's father's. "And this might not even be for that long. If your dad gets better, you could be back home with him before August."

Piper didn't miss the distinction: *if*, not *when*.

The chemo wasn't working, her father was growing weaker, and clearly no one thought he would recover—not even his own sister—because if they did, Aunt Eva would be saying *when*. *When* he got better. Not *if*.

Piper's aunt bit her bottom lip. "Aren't you at least a *little* excited to see your mother? It's been what—seven years?"

"Why would I be excited to see some snooty workaholic who's never cared about me?"

Now it was Aunt Eva's turn to blow out a breath.

Piper's mother, once a renowned scientist, had grown obsessed with what she called a "series of metaphysical

anomalies" at Mallory Estate while pregnant with Piper. The obsession continued—and strengthened—after Piper's birth. Sophia Peavey spent nearly every waking hour there, falling deep into her research, neglecting her family, and eventually moving back to the estate when Piper was four. Fast-forward another year, and she'd published a paper on the estate that had made her the laughingstock of her industry and cost Sophia her career and family. She hadn't even filed for custody during the divorce. Her obsession with Mallory Estate continued, and she was apparently fine with visitation rights only. Not that she'd ever visited.

"I guess I'm just not that excited to spend the summer with a parent who has forgotten every single one of my birthdays," Piper said. "Would it have killed her to send a card?"

Meanwhile, Grandma Mallory *always* remembered, *always* arrived bearing an expertly wrapped gift—usually a new book for Piper's collection—and *always* asked about Piper's life. *How's school? What are you learning? Anything exciting happen this past year?* It wasn't riveting conversation, but at least she cared enough to check in.

The car rolled to a stop, gravel crunching beneath the tires. Piper peered out the window.

The house—no, mansion—was ridiculous. Nearly every window had a box of flowers beneath it, and if it didn't have a window box, it had a balcony. Several steps led to a landing

beneath a portico, where a golden knocker shaped like a butterfly was mounted below the white door's peephole. Two potted decorative trees framed the entrance. Someone had pruned them into a swirling shape that looked an awful lot like an elongated green poop emoji.

Piper's lip curled. She'd rather be at the hospital, which was really saying something.

She shoved the car door open and slid from the vehicle. It was cool for late June, and she shouldered her backpack and folded her arms across her T-shirt.

"I still think you should have packed more," Aunt Eva said, lifting a small duffel from the trunk.

Refusing to accept that her summer plans were anything more than temporary, Piper had packed only ten days' worth of clothing (and books). Within ten days, her father's upcoming round of chemo would be over, and Piper had been certain he'd be returning home—and that she'd be able to return with him. Now, however, those assumptions seemed foolish.

"I'll be fine," she said, adjusting the brim of her beloved Yankees baseball cap.

"Do you want me to see you in?"

"I'm twelve, Aunt Eva. I can handle it."

"Great. I fly out tomorrow morning, and I have so much packing to do still." She planted a kiss on Piper's forehead and handed her the duffel. "Love you, Peavey. You need anything,

just give me a ring." Aunt Eva slid into the driver's seat, then lowered the passenger window and called out, "Just remember I might not pick up right away. This account is . . . well . . . I'm going to be busy. But I *will* check for messages from you, and I *will* call you on the weekends. Promise."

Piper nodded, and the car rolled off.

Only after the car was gone did she check her phone and see that she didn't have cell service. Maybe the estate would have a landline. It sure looked old enough to. And if not, she'd get on the Wi-Fi to text or e-mail if she needed to reach anyone. This place would have internet, right? She couldn't imagine that her "obsessed with history" grandmother and "obsessed with metaphysics" mother would be able to do their jobs very well without Internet access. Not that her mother had a job . . .

Stuffing her phone into her backpack, Piper climbed the front steps. She stared at the knocker. A troubling sensation pinched between her ribs. Fear, maybe. No. Not much scared Piper aside from caves, total and complete darkness, and (obviously) cancer. This felt more like nerves. Despite what she'd told Aunt Eva, Piper was anxious—perhaps even excited—to see her mother.

Maybe some time together would change things. Her mother would see how much she'd missed and admit that leaving had been a mistake. Grandma could help convince her to move back to the bungalow with Piper and her father,

and everything would be the way it was supposed to be: the three of them living together. Not separated and estranged and barely talking.

Piper realized she was playing with her necklace, and tucked the heart-shaped locket beneath her shirt. Then she lifted the knocker and let it fall with a cold, harsh *thunk*. Barely a second later, the door lurched open.

It was not her mother in the doorway, or even her grandmother.

It was a boy.

He had bronze skin and short-cropped dark hair, and he was wearing a gray zip-up hoodie, worn jeans, and a pair of beat-up sneakers. In one hand, he held a gleaming golden spyglass—the collapsing kind that pirates and privateers used.

"Piper Peavey?" he said with a grin. "We've been expecting you."

Chapter Two

Beware the White Persian

The boy looked about Piper's age, and he held his hand out, waiting for her to shake it. She merely blinked, dumbfounded. Finally Piper stepped from the stoop and into the foyer, squeezing past the boy, who reluctantly lowered his arm.

The foyer opened into a grand entry hall, where a second boy—maybe nine or ten years old—stood at the base of a sweeping staircase. What on earth were two kids doing at her grandmother's house? Piper avoided their curious eyes and took in the room.

Several stories overhead, rugged oak beams stretched the length of the ceiling. Wrought-iron lanterns hung from these joists, casting trapezoids of bright light on the gleaming hardwood floor. Expensive-looking statues stood against the

walls and exotic potted plants were sprinkled throughout the space, some as tall as trees; mirrors in gilded frames made everything look bigger and brighter. On the far wall, a set of French doors led outside to a furnished patio.

It was the most impressive room Piper had ever seen, and it was only the entry hall. She'd remembered Mallory Estate being fancy, but this was a whole other level.

"Um, I'm here to stay with my mom and grandmother; nobody mentioned they'd have other guests." She felt for her locket, staring at the children.

The boy who'd answered the door frowned. "We're not guests. Your mother started fostering about five years ago."

"I'm sorry," Piper said, jabbing at her ear with a finger, "but I thought you said *fostering*."

"That's right. Mrs. Peavey took us in. I'm Julius Gump and that's Kenji Naoki." He gestured toward the stairs.

"Hi!" the boy said with an enthusiastic wave. He had shaggy black hair and a toothy smile, and he was wearing a denim jacket over a plain tee and navy gym shorts.

Piper couldn't return his greeting.

The woman who had deserted her and her father— who had vanished and refused to make contact for all those years—suddenly cared about parenting? And not just for one child, but for two! Two children who weren't Piper. She blinked rapidly, fighting back tears.

"I was told to show you to your room," the older

boy—Julius—continued, collapsing his spyglass. He seemed to have noticed that Piper was on the verge of a meltdown, and was taking extreme efforts to look anywhere but at her eyes.

"Where's my mom?" Piper asked.

"Busy. She said she'll see you at dinner."

That sounded about right. She'd avoided Piper almost her entire life. Why change now?

"What about my grandmother?"

"She went out a week ago and hasn't returned yet." Julius shrugged, as though adults routinely disappeared from Mallory Estate and this was not at all cause for concern. Now Piper *really* hoped she could find a landline or get on the Wi-Fi. She needed to update Aunt Eva.

"This way." Julius turned, but Kenji still blocked the staircase, staring at Piper like she was some type of apparition.

"She's a person, not a tree frog," Julius snapped. "Can you go help Camilla?" He pointed his spyglass down the western hall, and Kenji scrammed.

"Who's Camilla?"

"Only the best twelve-year-old cook you'll ever meet," Julius said with a smile.

Piper gaped. Her mother was fostering three children. *Three*, not two. Desperate to talk about *anything* else, Piper gestured at her front and asked, "Tree frog? Really?" She was wearing black shorts, a white tee, and her Yankees cap, which

13

was such a deep navy, it was practically black. If anything, she was a penguin, assuming you could overlook her strawberry-blond hair.

"Your backpack is lime green, and it made me think of a tree frog. Besides, it made Kenji clear out."

There, Piper couldn't argue. She looked the way Kenji had run off—to the left, down a long hallway with an oriental rug. Oak doors and dimly glowing sconces lined the walls. To Piper's right was another hallway, seemingly identical to the first.

"What's down these?"

"The west wing," Julius said, pointing after Kenji, "holds the kitchen, dining hall, and library. The east wing has a bunch of fancy rooms that no one ever uses—billiards room, music room, smoking room. . . . Not that anyone here smokes. There's also a sitting room that we practice in sometimes."

Before Piper could ask, *Practice what?* Julius was rambling on.

"Mrs. Mallory's office is at the end of the hall, in the turret. It's completely off-limits—the whole turret, plus her chambers on the second floor. Your mother's chambers on that floor are off-limits too." He considered this for a second and added, "Best to just consider the entire second floor restricted. Come on, your room's this way."

Julius took the stairs two at a time, and Piper huffed after him, backpack digging into her shoulders and duffel

bumping her calves. They climbed straight past the second floor. At the third, Julius turned left down another lengthy hall. Piper paused on the landing to catch her breath. It was darker up here. There were fewer windows, and the entry hall lanterns now dangled beneath the landing, lighting only the lower levels.

Piper peered over the railing, mesmerized by how the staircase she'd just climbed spiraled away. Maybe this was why her mother had left. She'd tried to adjust to life at the bungalow, but she'd grown up with dining halls and libraries and frivolous smoking rooms that no one used. She was used to luxury. Nothing could compete with Mallory Estate.

Piper turned to follow Julius and froze. Just ahead, sitting in the middle of the carpet where the hallway began, was a white Persian cat. A leather collar studded with diamonds was clasped around its neck, and its fluffy tail twitched back and forth as it blinked its yellow eyes at Piper.

She crouched down, where she could make out the name WOLFE on a gold nameplate that hung from the pet's collar. Nothing about the animal seemed very beastlike. For starters, it was a house cat, not a wolf, and as it stretched its front legs, pawing at the carpet, Piper could see that its claws had been trimmed so short that she doubted it hunted, not even the mice that surely scampered around an estate this old. Given the style of its collar, it probably ate out of a crystal goblet.

Piper moved to scratch Wolfe behind the ears, but the

cat bared its teeth and hissed viciously. She yanked her hand back.

"That's the Persian," Julius called from farther down the hall. "Don't take it personally; he hates everyone. Also, he's a spy."

Piper stood slowly. "A spy?"

Julius nodded like he'd just made a very reasonable statement. "He stalks around the grounds, watching us, and he reports everything back to Mrs. Peavey and Mrs. Mallory."

"That's ridiculous." Piper barked out a laugh. "He's a *cat*."

"That's what we've always thought, but lately he's been summoning Mrs. Peavey when we get out of line."

"You're kidding." Piper scrunched her face up skeptically.

"Just wait. Next time you're someplace you're not supposed to be—like sneaking a peek at your mom's chambers on the second floor—the Persian will appear. He'll look at you, and blink his yellow eyes, and within minutes, Mrs. Peavey will show up and escort you back to your room or . . . wherever you should be."

Piper regarded the cat, which had just finished grooming a section of fur and was now hacking on a hair ball. There was no way this thing was a spy.

"Go ahead and test the theory later," Julius said with an indifferent shrug. "I'm not lying." He turned and continued to lead the way. Piper followed.

They proceeded to the end of the hall, where Julius

turned the doorknob of a gleaming oak door. "Here we are."

Piper glanced over her shoulder. The white Persian was sitting upright now, studying her, head cocked to the side in a very humanlike manner.

She shuddered and followed Julius into the room.

Chapter Three

Amplifiers and Affinities

There was a balcony. And a private bathroom. And a four-poster bed—the kind with a billowy, sheer canopy on top that Piper had only seen in movies. There was even a sitting area in one corner, in case the chairs on the balcony didn't strike her fancy.

"Are all the bedrooms like this?" she asked, gaping.

"Mine is, and I'm right next to you. Actually, I think every room on the backside of the house has the same floor plan." Julius opened the French doors to the balcony and stepped out. A dewy coolness hit Piper's cheeks as she followed.

Standing on the stone balcony, she got her first view of the elaborate grounds of Mallory Estate.

The slate surface of the patio directly below them was littered with chairs and chaise longues and wrought-iron

tables with glass tops. Several benches waited along the patio's edges, resting beneath the shade of maples and cherry trees whose blossoms lay trampled at the foot of their trunks. Next to each bench, a potting barrel overflowed with flowers and greenery. To the left of the patio were tennis courts, and to the right a worn, whitewashed carriage house.

But straight ahead, where the patio ended, so did the color.

Piper stared. Two beastly statues flanked several stone steps that led down into the dead garden. Piper thought the statues might have been lions once, lounging with their hind legs tucked beneath them and their front limbs stretched out, but it was impossible to tell, because they'd lost their heads over the years. A row of massive oak trees stretched straight ahead, away from the steps, their bare, blackened limbs clawing at the overcast sky. Dead leaves swirled by their roots.

Beyond this alley of oaks, dirt pathways snaked and twisted, cutting between statues covered in moss and rot, and framing murky pools of water that were filled with algae and other growth. What remained of the garden's flower beds were a tangle of dead weeds and brambles, and the hedges that separated sections of the sprawling garden appeared to be no more than a knotted wall of dead brush. Even the rock wall that made up the outer perimeter of the garden was crumbling. A latticework of shriveled ivy covered the stones.

"It's hideous," Piper said, shivering.

"Is it?" Julius passed her his spyglass. It felt ridiculous in

her hands. They were on a balcony, not the high seas. "Go on, look through it," he urged.

Reluctantly, Piper brought the spyglass to her eye and gasped.

"Not so dead after all, huh?"

Through the spyglass, the garden had transformed.

Brilliant ivy climbed the surrounding rock walls, and the row of oaks was in full bloom. Green leaves sprang from each of the trees' ancient branches, leaving the dirt path beneath sheltered in shadow. The grass was clipped short and even. The hedges trimmed and sculpted. Each flower bed was a rainbow of color. Each statue impeccably clean. The pools of water held nothing but a few flowering lily pads, their surfaces otherwise gleaming and clear. Some pools doubled as fountains, their surfaces rippling from the moving water. And it wasn't lions guarding the entry, as Piper had first theorized, but two stags, their golden antlers scraping at the sky.

Everything was so well maintained. Looking it over again, she noticed a new detail: the paths that wove through the garden didn't meander pointlessly. They formed a shape: the outline of a butterfly, just like the door knocker she'd rapped on the estate's front steps.

Piper lowered the spyglass and the dead, decaying garden stretched before her. She brought the spyglass up and the garden was again teeming with life.

"Is this some sort of trick?" she asked, examining the

spyglass. Was there a picture taped over the end? It had to be a prank. She turned the instrument over, finding nothing suspicious.

"It's an amplifier," Julius said matter-of-factly.

"An amplifier?"

"Yeah. To amplify, intensify, make stronger."

"I know what 'amplify' means. But a spyglass should show you things close up, like a pair of binoculars. This *changed* the garden." She shook the spyglass vigorously. "It looked alive. Tended to. *Perfect.*"

"It *is* perfect. The spyglass shows the truth."

Piper scanned the grounds with her bare eyes. The garden was definitely dead. Either she was missing something, or Julius was messing with her.

"It strengthens my affinity," he went on, taking the spyglass from her. "What's yours?"

"What the heck is an affinity?"

Julius frowned. "Your ability. My affinity is sight, or more specifically, being able to see the anomalies left behind after a spell has been performed. Without the spyglass, I can only see traces of these anomalies, pockets. They look fuzzy around the edges. Sometimes they even vibrate. But when I look through the spyglass, the amplifier shows me the truth. It reveals what was *before*. A long time ago, someone hid this garden, locked it away. Mrs. Mallory wants us to get inside. There's something valuable in there that she—"

"Hold on. Back up. *Spells?*" Piper gaped. "Like hocus-pocus, abracadabra, presto?"

Julius laughed. As if *she* were the one being ridiculous.

"No, that's fake stuff, like when you hire a magician to put on a show at a birthday party. I'm talking about the magi. Mrs. Mallory and Mrs. Peavey have spent the last decade trying to get into that garden. They started taking in kids like me recently—children with affinities—teaching us to strengthen our abilities with the use of an amplifier. That's why you were invited to live here. You're a magi too."

"No way," Piper said firmly. "I'm here because my father is . . . busy this summer. I've never heard of amplifiers or affinities before in my life!" She staggered off the balcony and collapsed on the bed. Suddenly all she could think about was what her own mother had grown obsessed with; her dad called it "metaphysical anomalies."

Julius had used that same word.

Anomalies.

Magic.

It was too much.

It wasn't possible.

This was the real world, which was logical and boring and had rules.

Rule #1: Cancer is treated with radiation therapy and chemotherapy.

Rule #2: The treatment *might* kill the cancer, but it will

definitely kill all your father's hair and make him weak, fatigued, and nauseous in the process.

Rule #3: Adults will try to shield you from what's happening because "you're only twelve," ignoring the fact that this is *your* father, and at the very least, you deserve to know what's going on.

Rule #4: Friends won't know how to act around you anymore. They'll get awkward and quiet, or smother you with pity and questions, or simply pull away because it's too much for them. As if it isn't a lot for *you*!

Rule #5: Worst of all, even if your father does everything right, the cancer might still win.

Piper hated all these rules, but they were the way of things. She wished they weren't. She *longed* for things like magic to be real, because then she could turn back time, make sure the doctors caught the cancer at such an early stage that her father stood a chance. No, she would cast a spell and eliminate the cancer altogether.

But that was fantasy. What Julius was talking about was *fantasy*.

"So where's your dad this summer?" Julius asked, joining her on the bed.

She considered telling him, but she just couldn't bear it. It was always the same when people learned about her father's situation. The awkward silence, followed by questions, then pity. (See Rule #4.)

"He's . . . traveling for work," she said.

"Oh." A pause. "Are you okay? You look kinda pale."

Piper snorted. "You just told me my mom and grandma are running a foster home for magically gifted children."

"Exactly." Julius looked pleased that she'd followed.

"Ugh, this isn't happening," she groaned, rolling face-first into a pillow. "I fell asleep in my aunt's car. We're still driving here and I'm dreaming in the back seat."

"Nope. This is very much real. Also: you definitely have an affinity."

"I think if I had magical abilities, I would know about them," Piper said.

"They could be dormant. Some of us knew our affinities before coming to Mallory Estate, but I didn't. Mrs. Mallory brought me in and helped me unlock it. Maybe you're the same." Piper raised her brows, skeptical. Julius exhaled. "After I've used my spyglass to find the true form of something, I can loan the amplifier to other magi and they'll be able to see what I did. The fact that you could see the garden—the hidden version—proves you're not a hollow."

"A hollow?" Piper asked.

"Someone empty. Without an affinity. Non-magi."

"Non-magi are empty? That sounds kinda elitist," Piper pointed out.

"I didn't come up with the term," Julius said defensively.

Piper touched her locket through her shirt and took a

deep breath. "Okay, so let's say I have some affinity, but it's dormant or whatever. Would there be any signs?"

"I thought something was wrong with my eyesight," Julius admitted. "There was always this fuzziness; certain things blurred. I figured I needed glasses, but eye doctors would always say my vision was perfect. I was so excited when the state placed me here—a rich foster parent meant I might finally be able to see a specialist, figure out what was wrong. Then Mrs. Mallory told me about affinities. She gave me the spyglass and showed me how to use it and explained everything about magi. We're very rare."

"I need to talk to my grandma," Piper said. *So I can put an end to this absurd prank,* she added mentally.

"She's not here right now, remember?"

"My mother, then."

"You'll see her at dinner. And don't you dare go searching her out before then. I'll get basement duty for letting someone disturb her." Julius clacked the spyglass shut, looking worried. "I have to go help the others in the kitchen now. But I'll see you later." He ran off without a backward glance.

Piper rolled onto her back and stared at the bed's canopy. Was *this* why her mother left? Not because the bungalow couldn't live up to Mallory Estate, but because Piper and her father were hollows? Had she chosen magic over family?

No, that was ridiculous. Magic wasn't real. Julius was telling her some elaborate story for kicks. He probably

did this to every new kid who came to the estate, but she wouldn't fall for it. As soon as she talked to her mother, she'd be able to confirm that everything he'd said about amplifiers and affinities was bogus.

Movement by the door caught her eye.

The Persian sat on the threshold, its head tilted in that uncomfortably human manner.

How long had it been there? Had it overheard her conversation with Julius?

It's just a cat, she reminded herself. *Even if it heard the conversation, it wouldn't understand any of it.*

She strode to the door and shut it in the animal's face.

Chapter Four

Anomalies of the Past

Shortly after her parents divorced, when Piper was exactly four and a half years old, Atticus Peavey had taken her to the aquarium.

Piper had said she wanted to go fishing for her half birthday, but it was early December, and snowing, so the aquarium was the next best thing. Atticus packed a lunch, buckled Piper into her car seat, and, like any sensible parent, drove two hours south to the Mystic Aquarium in the middle of a snowstorm. (This was not sensible at all when it came to safety. It was, however, quite sensible when it came to placating a young girl whose parents had just gotten divorced.) It helped that Atticus Peavey, who ran a construction business most of the year, plowed roads for the town during the winter. He was quite used to driving in sloppy, wintery conditions.

The drive took a bit longer than the expected two hours, because most people on the road did not have the same confidence that Atticus did driving in snow. Piper remembered her father grumbling in the front seat, saying things like, "It's just a dusting, people," and "Truly, the plow just went by. You can go faster than that." But every time he smiled at her in the rearview mirror, not an ounce of annoyance graced his features.

Atticus Peavey had a beautiful smile. At least until his diagnosis five years later. But that day at the aquarium, he smiled plenty. As they stared at penguins and ogled jellyfish. As they explored the touch tank and watched beluga whales feeding. Atticus didn't see the strange pair of security guards lurking just a few paces behind him and Piper, always just a step in the shadows, or he'd have been smiling less frequently.

Piper noticed them, but only in a *those men are interested in all the animals we are!* way. Not in a *those men have aquarium uniforms but no name badges* way. She was four and a half, after all. She didn't have reason to distrust anyone, except maybe her mother.

When they'd seen every last exhibit, Atticus brought Piper to the gift shop and told her she could pick out one stuffed animal to take home. "Just don't wander," he warned.

Piper nodded, but soon she was at the end of the stuffed animals display and the start of a wall of books—picture

books about all the animals they'd just seen. Surely it would be okay if she looked at the books.

That was when she heard talking.

"Yeah, she's the one. See the aura around her?"

Piper looked over her shoulder. Across the small gift shop, behind a display of beach toys, she could make out the two odd security guards. The skinnier one was looking at her through a pair of binoculars. *Strange,* she thought. *They liked all the animals we did, and now they like these books, too?*

"Let's do it now," the skinny guard said. "Quickly." He walked one way around the display of sand toys while his friend walked the other. He reached for a pair of handcuffs dangling from his belt, which Piper found odd. She thought only police officers carried handcuffs.

Suddenly Piper remembered conversations she'd had with her father about bad people—strangers who lured kids into cars with candy or puppies or sometimes even by force. "Dad?" she called, turning in circles. But she couldn't see him anymore. She'd wandered too far. The guards were halfway to her now, and moving quickly.

She ran, panicked, and collided with the display of stuffed animals. They rained down in an avalanche of plushness— dolphins and belugas and sea turtles and penguins—burying her there in the middle of the store.

Through a crack in the animals, Piper could see the men closing in. She clamped her eyes shut and squeezed

her knees, trying to become as small as possible.

"Where'd she go?"

"I don't know. She was right here!"

"Piper?" Atticus called out.

"We gotta go," the first guard mumbled.

Footsteps leaving. Others coming.

Piper cracked open an eye. The guards were gone and now she could make out a pair of familiar work boots drawing nearer. The person wearing them bent down, and Atticus's face peeked through a crack in the stuffed animals.

"Piper," he said disappointedly.

She shoved to her feet, stuffed animals toppling aside. "It was an accident."

"I know. Did you pick one?"

She grabbed the nearest—a penguin.

"Okay. Help me clean this up and then we can buy . . ." Atticus looked at the penguin.

"Carl," Piper said matter-of-factly.

"Nice to meet you, Carl. Now let's get your penguin family back in their bin."

Piper went to work, and her father went back to smiling, and she never thought about the guards again. Not until today, on the four-poster bed at Mallory Estate, as she reflected on Julius's explanation of affinities.

She shook her head. This was dumb. There was nothing magical about those men or the way she'd hidden. Julius's

trick with the spyglass was simply too good, his acting so convincing that she was looking for magic where there wasn't any.

She grabbed her phone and drafted a quick e-mail to Aunt Eva, letting her know that she'd been shown to a room, but that Grandma Mallory wasn't even at the estate. Then she tried to get on the Wi-Fi. There was only one network— *MalloryEstate*—and it was locked. Grumbling, Piper tossed her phone aside and collapsed backward.

Before her head even hit the quilt, the door to her room burst open.

"Knock much?" Piper cried out, jolting upright.

The girl standing in the doorway was Piper's age, with brown skin and dark hair that was gathered in a tight bun at the top of her head. The few curls that had escaped the elastic corkscrewed wildly. She wore flip-flops, a denim skirt, and a T-shirt that said THE SASS IS STRONG WITH THIS ONE in the Star Wars font. In her right hand, she held a gold coin. No, *held* wasn't the right word, Piper reasoned, because the girl was making the coin dance—passing it from knuckle to knuckle like a casino gambler.

"Julius sent me to get you," the intruder said. "It's dinnertime."

"I'm Piper Peavey," Piper said, holding out her hand.

"I know. We all do." The other girl tucked the coin into her skirt pocket and looked at her nails, bored. "Are you

coming? If they burn something while I'm gone, I will lose it."

"You're Camilla," Piper said, remembering how Julius had mentioned a twelve-year-old chef.

The girl gave a very exaggerated sigh. "Yeah, Camilla Cortez. And let me just get this out of the way: you'll see Julius later and he'll say, 'Camilla really isn't so bad once you get to know her,' but I am. I'm not nice. I'm not looking to make friends and I definitely don't want to be yours. Princess Piper who's come to live at her grandmother's estate, thinking she's better than everyone and can beat us to the prize?" Camilla rolled her eyes. "Pu-lease."

Piper had no clue what prize Camilla was even referencing.

"If you don't have to keep this place running like the rest of us . . ." The girl let the thought die, but her lips curled slightly, and the look she was giving Piper was pure fire.

"Spite," Piper said. "It should have said 'spite.'"

Camilla frowned. "What should have said 'spite'?"

"Your shirt." Piper brushed past a speechless Camilla and into the hall.

At the bottom of the stairs, Piper paused. When Julius had shooed off Kenji earlier, the boy had run down the hall that Julius said also held the dining room. To the left. But she'd been facing the stairs then, not coming down them, which meant now she had to go . . .

"To the right," Camilla snipped, catching up to her.

Piper headed right. Her sneakers were soundless on the rug; Camilla's flip-flops made a muted *thwick-thwack, thwick-thwack* as they walked. Passing a set of French doors that led to the library, Piper caught a quick glimpse of towering bookshelves and work desks with small desk lamps and upholstered chairs.

"What are you doing in the hall?" Camilla snapped. Piper looked up to see Julius waiting to greet them. "I told you to make sure the ham came out at exactly seven. If it dries out, not even the honey glaze will save it."

"The ham is fine," he said pointedly. To his left, a set of double doors were propped open, revealing a grand dining hall with polished floors and velvet curtains of rich emerald that framed floor-to-ceiling windows looking out onto the patio. A table large enough to seat thirty (but set only for two) was positioned in the center of the room. To Piper, he added, "I see you met Camilla."

"Unfortunately," Camilla mumbled before Piper could say anything.

"Don't let her scare you," Julius insisted. "She's really not so bad once you get to know her."

Camilla cocked an eyebrow at Piper, as if to say, *Did I call it, or what?* and for the briefest moment a smile spread over her lips. Then she seemed to remember that she was set on despising Piper and flattened her smile into a grimace,

huffed past the dining hall, and disappeared through a small, unimpressive door at the end of the hall.

"She told me you'd say that," Piper said to Julius. He shrugged awkwardly. "Where'd she run off to?"

"That," Julius said, pointing to the door Camilla had taken, "leads to a corridor that accesses the kitchen—and Camilla is in her element in the kitchen. It's her happy place."

"Yeah, she sure seemed thrilled to glaze the ham," Piper said sarcastically.

"Everyone's on edge this week. Things have been a little . . . off." He scratched the back of his neck and became very interested in the wallpaper.

"Why?"

"You should really sit down. Mrs. Peavey hates waiting. At least, she's been super impatient this past week."

"She's in there already?" Piper hadn't seen anyone at the table, and her pulse quickened as she checked the dining hall again. She wasn't sure she was ready to meet her mother. What do you say to someone you haven't seen in seven years?

"No, of course not. When she arrives, she'll expect dinner to be served immediately. Now, please, will you just go in before . . ."

Julius's face paled. His body went very still. His eyes widened.

"Good evening, Mrs. Peavey," he said, gaze fixed over Piper's shoulder. "Dinner is almost ready."

Striding up the hall, heels silent on the rug, was Piper's mother.

Piper's heart beat wildly in her chest. She stood straighter, pushed her shoulders back.

Will she recognize me? Has she missed me?

Piper couldn't help it. She should hate her mother for leaving—and for years she had—but now that she was standing just feet away from the woman, Piper found herself smiling, desperate for Sophia Peavey to like her.

Polished.

That was the only word Piper could come up with for her mother. From her red hair (smoothed into an elegant French twist) to her clothing (wine-colored blouse and dark pencil skirt), all the way down to her heels (shiny black patent leather), there wasn't a crooked hem or stray thread or loose hair out of place. She looked more like a model than a parent. Piper didn't feel any motherly warmth from her—not for herself, or for Julius, either.

She felt foolish, grinning there like a puppet, and wiped the giddy smile from her face.

Nothing about this woman looked like the one pictured inside Piper's locket. That woman smiled; the woman before Piper kept her lips pursed tightly. Piper had never realized how a smile could change someone, bring life to their skin and joy to their eyes. She should have. She'd noticed how these things had been slowly leached from her father. But

until now, she hadn't put together that it was his smile that had truly caused the change. That these days, when her father smiled, it was only an attempt at one, and in that attempt, the joy didn't reach his eyes. When he stopped smiling altogether, would he look like this woman before Piper? A soulless stranger?

Sophia Peavey stopped an arm's length from Piper and looked her up and down.

"Why are you not sitting?" she asked. Her voice was cold and distant, her green eyes rimmed with flecks of gold.

"What?" Piper said, which was silly, because she'd heard her mother just fine. She simply couldn't believe that after not speaking for so long, *this* was the first thing her mother chose to say to her. She'd expected a hug. Or at least a kind hello.

"Sitting," Sophia drawled, accentuating the *t*'s with annoyance. "I'm hungry. You should already be at your place."

"Yes, right this way," Julius muttered, and he shoved Piper into the dining room with a palm between her shoulders.

Chapter Five

Small Talk After Seven Years

Piper had only two real memories of her mother from their time as a family of three.

The first was a nice one—a moment that always made her chest ache when she recalled it.

Her mother was already spending most of her time at Mallory Estate, but that afternoon she was home, sorting through her closet. Piper, roughly three, had no idea this was because Sophia would soon be leaving for good. She'd simply been content to play peekaboo from behind her mother's hanging dresses, teetering around in a pair of Sophia's heels.

Sometimes in the dark corner of the closet, Piper felt like a different person. A princess lost in a cave. No, a knight off to fight a dragon!

"Piper?" her mother called. "Where'd you go?"

The dresses parted, revealing her mother. She looked through Piper—more at the back wall than anything else—and shifted through more clothes. "Piper?"

Piper giggled to herself, uncertain how her mother had overlooked her, then burst from between the dresses. "Boo!" she yelled.

Her mother jumped, a look of surprise on her face, then laughed. "Oh, that is lovely," she said, eyeing the ensemble Piper had donned: a pair of red heels, a sun hat with a floppy brim that she'd found on the floor, and a small leather purse that she was wearing around her front like a necklace.

"I thought I'd lost you," Sophia said.

"Boo!" Piper repeated. "I'm right here!"

Again, her mother smiled.

The other memory was closer to the divorce, just days before it was finalized. Piper had come to her parents' bedroom early that morning. Her father was still in his pajamas. Her mother sat at the edge of the bed, back to the doorway, with a suitcase at her feet.

Piper pushed the door open a crack, and her parents glanced briefly in her direction. She froze, half hidden behind the doorframe, but they must not have seen her, because they resumed their conversation.

"You don't have to do this," Atticus said to Sophia.

"I do."

"You and I both know there's no way that is actually true."

Sophia shook her head. "I don't expect you to understand."

There was an awkward silence.

"What about Piper?" her father asked.

"I have to do this," Sophia said firmly, not answering Atticus's question. "So that I can come home." Then she picked up the suitcase and left the room, flinching when she found Piper spying from the hallway. "It's early," she said to her. "Go back to bed." Then she kissed Piper's forehead and left.

In the coming years Piper would revisit this memory, certain she'd heard her mother wrong. *I have to do this. This isn't my home,* she probably said. Because her home was never Atticus and Piper. How could it be, when she'd abandoned them and never looked back? How could she have ever loved them when she made leaving look so easy?

This was the moment Piper was thinking about as Julius half guided, half pushed her to a seat at the end of the long mahogany dining table. Crystal chandeliers cast flashes of light on the glossy surface. Piper slumped into her chair. Her mother slid gracefully into her own at the other end of the table. It seemed like a football field separated them.

Pacing at the edge of the room, tail leaving long white hairs on the velvet curtains, was the Persian.

The doors at the rear of the dining hall burst open and Camilla and Kenji marched in. Camilla carried the first course—two bowls of golden butternut squash bisque—which

she set before Piper and Sophia. Kenji approached with a large decanter. It took Piper a minute to realize it was filled with wine.

"Um, I think I should have water," she whispered to him as he filled her glass.

"This is what Mrs. Peavey requested," he said, practically trembling. Wine sloshed in the decanter. Piper had the distinct feeling that if he spilled any, her mother wouldn't hesitate to assign him basement duty.

"Oh, that's fine, then," she said. "Don't worry about it." Kenji smiled meekly as he poured, and when he left, Piper moved the wineglass off her place mat.

At the other end of the table, Sophia picked up her spoon without so much as a glance in Piper's direction and began to eat. Stomach grumbling, Piper did the same. The bisque was delicious; creamy and thick and flavorful. It was hard to believe a bunch of schoolkids could cook this well.

"You found it okay, then?" Sophia said from across the table.

"What?"

"The estate. You found it easily?"

Mallory Estate was tucked away at the end of a quarter-mile gravel drive on a 120-acre plot of land, but Blackburn itself wasn't exactly hard to find. It was only two towns northwest of Piper's hometown. The driveway had been a bit hard to spot from the main road—crowded with growth and

lying in shadow—but Piper assumed her aunt had acquired detailed directions, because they'd arrived without incident.

"Yes, Aunt Eva brought me."

Sophia stared at Piper for an uncomfortably long beat.

"Evangeline. Remember her? Daddy's sister."

Sophia sighed as if this detail bored her, then set down her spoon. "Let me get a few ground rules out of the way. You are not allowed on the second floor or in the estate's turret. Dinner is served at exactly seven every day. This is the only meal I'll be taking with you."

"Every day or just to—"

"Just today," Sophia spat, the gold rimming her eyes practically flashing like fire. She took a long sip from her goblet and Piper sat deathly still, afraid to breathe too loudly. "After tonight, you will help prepare meals with the others, as well as complete routine chores. They'll fill you in on the details.

"You're on your own for breakfast and lunch, which should be eaten promptly at eight and noon. I will get those meals at my own leisure. Use the servant corridor to access the kitchen, and eat back there as well. I don't want to see you in the dining hall, nor do I want to see you around the house. If you're inside and have free time, make yourself a ghost. If you need to scream or run or do anything decidedly childlike"—her lip curled—"go outside. Curfew is nine p.m., after which you should be in your bedroom and no place else

41

for the remainder of the evening. Any questions?"

"What about the garden?"

Something came to an abrupt halt in the corner of Piper's vision. Julius. He was bringing in the next course. She wondered briefly if his trick with the spyglass would get him in trouble. Piper's mom didn't seem like the type who could appreciate a good prank.

"What about the garden?" Sophia's forefinger traced the rim of her goblet.

"It looks . . ." Piper glanced out the windows, to the blackened oak trees beyond the steps. "Dangerous. I heard there was a fire a long time ago, but . . . is it safe now? Can I explore it?"

"A fire is only dangerous when it's burning. Ash is harmless. I thought you were supposed to be bright."

Piper didn't know how her mother knew that her grades were exceptional. It wasn't as if she ever checked in or visited. Maybe Grandma Mallory updated her.

"Any other stupid questions?"

Piper felt a lump form in her throat. *Don't cry. Change the subject. Talk about something else.*

"Where's Grandma?" she managed.

"Out."

"Out where?"

"Attending to business. She might be held up for the rest of the summer."

"The entire summer?" From what Piper could remember, her grandmother's job as an archivist didn't involve a lot of travel. When she wasn't doing research from her office at the estate, she was at the Blackburn Historical Society in town. But even if she was held up there, it didn't make sense for her not to return home for a meal or shower every once in a while.

The Persian mewled from the edge of the room, and Sophia narrowed her eyes at Piper. "She's doing some research out of state," she clarified. "She'll be back when she's back."

Julius took Piper's soup bowl and slid a salad before her. At the opposite end of the table, Camilla did the same for Piper's mother. The Persian leaped onto the table, and Sophia scratched the pet behind the ears, then lowered her lips to its forehead and whispered sweetly.

Piper's blood went hot.

It wasn't just this one moment with the Persian—though it *was* infuriating to see her mother show more love and attention to a cat than her own daughter—it was all of it. A lifetime of being ignored, and being belittled over dinner, and the fact that the only parent she loved and wanted to be with was hours away at the hospital, slowly losing a fight with cancer, alone.

"So that's it?" she screeched. "That's all you have to say to me? Stay out of the turret and avoid the second floor and be invisible in the house? That's how I'm supposed to spend my summer?!"

Sophia went very still. When she raised her eyes to Piper, the Persian did the same; two sets of eyes—one green rimmed with gold, the other a brilliant yellow—stared at her for an uncomfortably long time. Then Sophia set her napkin on the table.

"I'm tired," she said blithely. "I'm going to bed."

"But this is only the second course," Piper protested.

Her mother said nothing, only stood and strode from the room, with the Persian padding after her clicking heels.

Piper stared at the open doors, certain her mother would reappear. Her lip trembled, and when it was clear Sophia wasn't returning, she pulled her locket from beneath her shirt and cracked it open.

The woman within was planting a kiss on a chunky baby's cheek while Atticus squeezed them both. Even mid-kiss, it was obvious the woman was smiling, so much so that she was practically laughing.

A tear trailed down Piper's cheek and landed in her lap.

"Way to go, princess," Camilla said. "All that work in the kitchen, and for what?"

But for all her sass, Camilla brought out the third course—roasted ham with a honey glaze and a side of sweet green beans—and when Piper found the strength to look up, she realized she wasn't alone. Julius, Camilla, and Kenji had all gathered at the table to eat with her.

"She's not usually like that," Kenji said.

Piper wasn't sure she believed him, but the moment felt so warm, so full, so positively pleasant compared to the courses with her mother, that she tucked her locket away and picked up her fork. She wasn't used to being seen like this, being included. Not at school, where she sat alone at lunch since Bridget had pulled away, and was always picked last for gym teams. Not at the hospital, where nurses and doctors moved around her like she didn't exist. Not even at home, where Atticus and Aunt Eva had begun making all his medical decisions without Piper, never giving her a say.

She smiled despite everything and stopped only when Camilla commented that the ham was a little dry and why did Piper think this was even remotely amusing?

It was a wonderful meal, all things considered.

Chapter Six

The Garden's Prize

When dinner was over, Piper helped clear the dishes. The kitchen was large enough to hold the entire first floor of the bungalow, and it had twice the number of appliances. There was a pair of double ovens, a walk-in freezer, two fridges, and racks hanging from the ceiling that held additional cookware and dried herbs. You could easily prep a dozen Thanksgiving meals in here.

"Thanks for coming to eat with me," Piper said as she wiped down the central counter.

Camilla shrugged. "It was Julius's idea. He's so nice it's sickening."

Julius blushed.

"Do you seriously have to cook my mom a three-course meal every night?" Piper asked. "And when and where do

you guys get to eat if she stays in the dining hall for the full meal?"

"We eat back here, between courses," Julius said.

"But we used to all eat together. And she used to cook with us," Kenji said, using a step stool to hang a skillet from the rack suspended above the counter. "She kinda took Camilla under her wing, taught her everything she knows."

"Your mom could be a chef at a five-star restaurant," Julius added, "but like I said, she's been acting strange lately."

"Really demanding," Kenji agreed. "Almost cruel."

Camilla straightened, hands on her hips. "Hey, not all of us mind having to tackle meal prep alone."

Julius rolled his eyes. "And not all of us want to be professional chefs."

"So she's only been terrible recently?" Piper asked. "Why?"

Camilla shrugged. "It's a lot of work to keep this place running. We all pitch in; she's probably just overwhelmed with your grandmother stepping out for so long."

Piper brushed some crumbs into the garbage and moved on to the stove top. Some of Camilla's honey glaze had dried on the burners. "You should say something. It's not right the way she's treating you."

The children shared a quick glance. "We can't say anything," Julius said.

"Did she threaten you? That's all the more reason. She

shouldn't be a foster parent. She's a terrible mother, and if you just tell the social worker or whoever checks in with you what's happening, I'm sure that—"

"Piper, cool it," Camilla interrupted. "Mrs. Peavey is great."

"And we're not going to say anything," Julius agreed, but Kenji's mouth quirked in a slant, like maybe he didn't fully agree.

"Why not?" Piper pressed. "Doesn't someone check in on you? Isn't that how foster care works? They should know what's going on here."

"No one checks in," Julius said. "Mrs. Mallory pulled a few strings or something. I'm not sure how, exactly, but we're lucky."

"Lucky?!" Piper practically screeched.

"I'm sure things will go back to normal once Mrs. Mallory returns," Camilla insisted. "Your mom's just . . . stressed."

Kenji frowned. "But what about—"

"We've talked about this," Julius said firmly. "We keep working together and stay focused on the garden. That's the only way forward."

"My mom's not stressed, she's a monster," Piper insisted. "And clearly unfit to be anyone's parent. What's the Wi-Fi password? I'm e-mailing my aunt and telling her everything."

"Only Mrs. Mallory and Mrs. Peavey know the password," Kenji answered.

"We've asked for it before, but they won't give it to us," Julius added.

Piper peered at them, trying to determine if they were lying.

"We understand," Camilla went on. "It's important that the garden remains a secret. And Mrs. Mallory doesn't want us slipping up, saying the wrong thing to the wrong person."

"People will come looking for it if we do," said Julius in a serious tone.

"For the garden?" Piper frowned. "Who cares about a dead garden?"

"Your grandma doesn't want anyone to know about the garden, period," Julius clarified. "If the truth about it got out ... If people knew what was inside ..." He bit his lip. "Like I said, we're really lucky she's trusted us to help her."

"What's in the garden?" Piper asked.

The kids shared a knowing look. Were they all in on Julius's spyglass trick? This was starting to feel very elaborate.

Julius nodded toward the door, and Piper followed him into the hall, Camilla and Kenji padding along beside them.

"The garden holds something too powerful to be trusted to hollows," Julius explained as they headed for the stairs. "So powerful that the High Order of Magi didn't even trust their own kind to use it wisely."

Piper cocked up a brow. "What?"

"An elixir of immortality," Julius whispered. "Whoever drinks it can live forever."

Piper examined them again, skeptical, but their expressions remained serious.

"And if we find it, we get adopted," Kenji said eagerly. "Imagine a permanent home here, at Mallory Estate!"

"Why would you want to live *here*?" Piper glanced at the sweeping staircase before them, shivering as her voice echoed in the lonely house. The place was so empty and big and . . . cold. Plus, her mother was the worst.

"I promise: it's not really that bad," Julius insisted. "We get to be ourselves here, don't have to hide our affinities. If you'd arrived before Mrs. Mallory left, you'd understand. You'd have seen how great your mom is."

They reached the landing and Piper paused, staring out the window that overlooked the garden. In the twilight glow it looked more skeletal than ever, like a graveyard of bones and weeds.

"Didn't you say my mom and grandma were these superpowerful magi? Can't they get this elixir themselves?"

"They've been trying," Kenji said.

"For years," Camilla added.

Julius nodded in agreement, tapping a thumb on the side of his spyglass. "The High Order of Magi *really* hid it. This was ages ago, around the Civil War. But one of the current HOM members recently tasked Mrs. Mallory with

extracting it, and she couldn't figure it out on her own. That's why the HOM helped pull strings in the foster care system, getting us placed here so we could help. I was first, about five years ago. Kenji and Camilla followed. You've been here about, what?" He glanced at them.

"Almost two years," Camilla answered.

"Three now for me," Kenji said.

"Why do these High Order people want the elixir out of the garden so badly?" Piper asked.

"To protect it. Think of how powerful a magic like that is!" Julius was staring at Piper as though she were brainless for not following. "In the wrong hands, it would be sold to the highest bidder. Or replicated and reproduced on a massive scale. People will only seek it out of greed!"

"But it sounds like it's protected just fine," Piper argued, feeling more confused than ever. "My mom and grandma can't get to it, and neither can you guys. If this is all true, the original High Order of Magi hid the elixir perfectly."

Camilla shook her head. "They left a back door, a way to access the garden."

"It *can* be found," Julius concluded. "And the HOM knows that magi artifact hunters are after the elixir, so we have to get to it first."

If extracting the elixir was so important, Piper didn't understand why the current members of the HOM weren't at Mallory Estate too, helping with the task instead of

entrusting it to a bunch of kids. But before she could ask this, Camilla's eyes narrowed. "And let me tell you right now, princess. You already have a family. I know your dad's dumped you here for the summer—Julius explained everything. It stinks, but you don't need a home like we do. So don't bother even *trying* to get into that garden."

"Come on, Camilla," Kenji groaned. "Don't be like that. We need all the help we can get. Especially with—"

"Fine. Try to get into the garden," Camilla said, cutting him off. "But if you make any progress, you better tell us. *We* need this. Me and Julius and Kenji. *We* should be the ones to find the elixir, not you."

And with that, Camilla turned and strode for her room.

At night, Mallory Estate sounded like a sleeping giant. The radiators clacked and rattled. The walls exhaled and groaned. When a toilet was flushed nearby, a whoosh of water moved through the pipes overhead, like blood pumping through veins.

Piper stared at the pale, sweeping canopy above her four-poster bed, Carl the penguin tucked beneath her arm. He'd faded greatly since being purchased at the aquarium, but Piper's love for him hadn't. Bridget said twelve was too big to sleep with a stuffed animal, but Bridget had been a crummy friend recently, and she didn't like reading, on top of everything else. How could Piper possibly care about the opinions of a friend-abandoning book hater?

What she cared about, in that moment, was what the kids had told her on the stairs.

An elixir of immortality.

Hidden in the garden.

Locked away because the world couldn't be trusted with it.

It sounded impossible. But so did magi and affinities and amplifiers, and everything the kids had told her had been in such detail; it was getting hard to believe they'd go to such lengths for a prank. If magi were real, then maybe magi artifacts were real too.

An elixir of immortality . . .

Piper pictured her father in the hospital. His halfhearted smile. His bald head. His frail, weakening body. The cancer was taking everything from him—from her—but an elixir could change all that. It could end Atticus's suffering and make him immortal.

Don't do this, Piper thought. Every time her father started another round of chemo or the doctors proposed a new treatment, she had let herself hope. And every time, she'd been disappointed. She couldn't do it again—believe there was a solution only to have her heart crushed. If no one had found a way into the garden after all this time, there was no way Piper would either. She didn't even have an affinity!

Then again, Julius had said that before he found his affinity, he'd thought something was wrong with his vision.

Piper sometimes felt like something was wrong with her, as a whole.

People would often stare at her, looking straight through her, as though she weren't there. The nurses did this all the time at the hospital. She'd ask how her father was doing or when he'd last eaten, and they'd gaze absentmindedly at her, then leave without answering. Other times people would do a double take, like her mother had that day Piper had played peekaboo in her closet.

Most recently, this had happened at school. Piper had shown up late to homeroom, and her teacher had glanced at the door when she walked in. Rather than reprimanding her as he usually did tardy students, he simply went back to taking attendance, so Piper proceeded to her desk. Then, when she called out "here" after he said her name, he literally flinched, staring at her as though her existence wasn't welcome.

She shook her head, feeling ridiculous. She was searching for moments of wrongness in her past when *everything* was wrong—her cruel and distant mother, her sick father, the fact that she was stuck at Mallory Estate for summer vacation.

She needed fresh air.

Piper slipped from her bed, grabbed a hoodie, and then padded to the French doors, floorboards creaking underfoot. Out on the balcony, the stone was cold against her bare feet. She folded her arms across her body, shivering.

The garden stretched out before her. Mist hung low, curling around statues, and the dead oaks glistened almost silver in the moonlight. Dried leaves skittered across the dirt paths. Piper observed them again, following their twists and curves. If she ignored the overgrown weeds, if she strained her eyes to follow the faded walkways, she could see the same butterfly shape she had through Julius's spyglass. The wings, the body, the head.

Something moved at the far end of the garden and she froze. From this distance, the Persian was little more than a speck of white fluff, but Piper watched it circle around the algae-covered pool that made up the butterfly's head. Without warning, the cat jerked toward the balcony. The distance between them seemed suddenly small as the animal's yellow eyes pierced through the night and locked with Piper's.

She drew back, stumbling into her bedroom and shutting the French doors. She stood there a moment, pulse pounding. Was it really out there—a cure for her father's suffering? If the garden held an elixir that could save Atticus, didn't Piper owe it to him to try to find it?

She climbed into bed and told herself not to get too excited. It was just a dead garden. . . .

Wasn't it?

Chapter Seven

Laundry Duty

Tuesday morning dawned golden, sunbeams hitting the bedsheets and warming Piper's face.

She dressed quickly, pulling on a pair of jean shorts and a T-shirt from a gymnastics competition two years earlier. It had been the last one she'd competed in.

"If you're quitting because of me, that's a really bad reason," her father had said.

"I'm just over it," ten-year-old Piper had replied with a shrug. The truth was that gymnastics wasn't cheap and Atticus's hospital bills were getting expensive—Piper had overheard him and Aunt Eva talking about how to stretch his budget—and really, what was the point? She could win every gold trophy and it wouldn't heal her father. All gymnastics was doing was taking her away from him, to all corners of the

state and even remote parts of New England every month.

Tucking her hair behind her ears, Piper pulled on her Yankees cap and made her way downstairs. In the entry hall, a set of grand French doors opened directly onto the patio, but she carried on to the kitchen, stomach growling. It was still spotless from last night's cleaning—and empty. Clearly, no one at Mallory Estate was an early bird, which suited Piper just fine. She wanted to get a look at the garden alone.

She scrambled an egg and cooked it in the microwave instead of on the stove (which Camilla probably considered a deadly sin). Then, after shoveling down her breakfast, she slipped out the kitchen's side door and onto the patio. The garden looked as dead as ever.

Because it is *dead,* she reminded herself.

Standing between the two headless stag statues, Piper angled her cap to avoid the morning sun, then descended the steps.

Nothing changed. The oak alley was still skeletal, the grass brittle and dry, and of *course* it was. She had to hand it to Julius and the others—they'd almost worn her down.

Piper passed through the oak alley. The dead branches cast a cobwebbed shadow of teeth and claws on the dirt. The path split eventually, branching out to create the butterfly's wings, and Piper followed one of the walkways past a rectangular pool. Several inactive fountain spouts were positioned throughout the water, protruding from the

algae-covered surface. In the center of the pool, three raised pedestals each held a statue of a woman wearing sweeping robes. Their golden finishes were dull, tarnished, and flaking. Piper backtracked to the main path and explored the other side of the garden, finding another rectangular pool with inactive fountain spouts and statues identical to the first.

The next time that Piper returned to the central path, her feet carried her north, away from the oak alley, the estate. This main walkway cut between the long rectangular pools she'd just explored. She could see them to the left and right, each stretching away from her, their weathered statues no larger than her thumb from this distance.

Soon she was approaching the pool that made up the butterfly's head. This was where she'd seen the Persian last night, she realized.

Like the others, this pool was stagnant and covered in algae, but there were no fountain spouts, only a pedestal in the pool's center. If a statue had once sat there, it was long gone. Piper dropped a pebble into the water and listened, but it was impossible to guess how deep the pool was.

A tiny *meow* at Piper's back sent her twisting. The Persian sat in the walkway, flicking its snow-white tail.

"Get out of here! Scram." She shooed the cat with her hands, then froze. Her mother was approaching. Sophia wore an ensemble almost identical to the one from yesterday, only today her shirt was emerald green.

"Why are you out here?" Sophia said, looking between Piper and the pool.

Piper frowned. "You didn't say the garden was off-limits."

"You should be inside with the others. It's laundry day."

Piper stared at her mother, certain this was some kind of joke. Then again, her mother had mentioned that Piper would need to help the others with chores.

"You're not moving," Sophia drawled, impatient.

A lump swelled in Piper's throat. She darted around Sophia and broke into a jog.

It was only when she was inside, searching out a set of stairs to the basement (because she hadn't seen a laundry room anywhere else in the estate and assumed it must be downstairs), that she remembered what Julius had said about the Persian. *Next time you're someplace you're not supposed to be, the Persian will appear. He'll look at you, and blink his yellow eyes, and within minutes, Mrs. Peavey will show up.*

Maybe the cat was a spy after all.

The stairs to the basement were located at the end of the western wing on the first floor, opposite the servant corridor that accessed the kitchen.

Piper took the dark, steep steps carefully, a hand gripped firmly on the banister. Her shoulder bumped something on the wall, causing it to jingle. A rack of rings, each set filled with a variety of keys—silver and gold, tarnished and dull. She carried on, eyes adjusting, until she was in the dank belly of Mallory Estate. There, she followed the chatter of buoyant voices to the laundry room. It had a low ceiling of pipes and cobwebs, and several industrial-size washers and dryers. Drying racks filled the rear of the room, where Julius was hanging delicate clothes, most of which appeared to be Sophia's fancy blouses and skirts. Camilla and Kenji were busy folding sheets and towels and organizing them into various piles.

Piper heard a *whoosh*, and several sheets of bedding fell from the ceiling—through a laundry chute—and landed in a bin beside the washers.

"Ugh, but we just finished the bedding," Camilla moaned.

"She's being purposely mean," Kenji grumbled. "I can't wait until Mrs. Mallory gets back."

"Do you guys need help?" Piper asked, stepping forward. Everyone looked up, finding her in the doorway. This was still new to Piper, getting people's attention. It was almost unsettling. "My mother sent me to help," she explained quickly.

Julius waved her toward the drying racks. "Where were you at breakfast?"

"Exploring the garden."

"You thought you could find a way in on your very first attempt?" Camilla scoffed as she shook wrinkles from a shirt.

"More like, this all sounds impossible, so I poked around, and *yup*, still seems impossible."

"Spoken like a true hollow," Camilla said. "Hey, maybe that's why your mom was so mean last night. Must be disappointing for your own kid to not have an affinity."

"Oh, she has an affinity," Julius said.

Piper sighed. "You guys can stop with the magi stuff now. It was a really elaborate story—I'll give you that—but it's getting old."

"We're not kidding," Julius said. "A magi will give off a white aura, almost like a glimmer. I saw yours with my spyglass the moment you stepped out of your aunt's car yesterday."

All Piper could think about were the aquarium guards. *See the aura around her?* Even still, she heard herself saying, "Right, sure."

"Why would we lie to you?" Julius asked. "I don't know what we have to do to make you believe us."

"I know," Kenji said, and he flipped the collar of his denim jacket. He vanished in a blur of brilliant light, then reappeared right before Piper. "Teleportation. A Naoki family specialty. My jacket's my amplifier."

Piper gaped. It had been easy to assume Julius's spyglass was doctored, but this? This was something else. There was no way to fake what Kenji had just done.

"Family specialty?" she asked numbly.

"Sometimes certain affinities stick within a family tree. My parents could teleport too. If they'd seen the Mack truck running the light, they'd have jumped straight out of the car and to safety. But I'm here, so clearly that didn't happen."

Piper had always thought that watching someone die slowly, like with her father, was the worst possible way to lose someone. But suddenly and unexpectedly, like Kenji had experienced, sounded just as terrible. The truth was there was no good way to lose someone. It was always awful.

"That sucks," she said to Kenji.

"Yeah," he agreed. "It does. I wish they could see this place. We lived on a busy block in West Hartford and couldn't safely use our affinities without hollows seeing. There should be more places like Mallory Estate—communal homes for magi."

Piper turned toward Camilla. "And you have . . . an affinity for cooking?" she asked.

"I wish!" The girl pulled a gold coin from her pocket—the same coin Piper had seen her move over her knuckles last night—and clenched it in her palm. When she opened her fist, the coin had become a stone. Camilla clenched and opened again. A ball of clay. Another squeeze and it was the coin again.

"You can transform things?" Piper asked, unable to take her eyes off Camilla's palm.

Camilla grinned proudly. "Anything inanimate. Otherwise I'd transform you into another washing machine so this would all go faster."

"Believe us now?" Julius asked.

Piper nodded, glancing between them. There was no denying it anymore: as impossible as it sounded, magi were most definitely real. There were three standing right in front of her.

"I still think you're wrong about me having an affinity," Piper said. "But you guys definitely have . . . something."

"Affinities," Julius corrected.

"Right."

"Maybe you can study with us," Kenji said hopefully. "Monday, Wednesday, and Friday mornings are for classes: Magi History, Concealment Studies, and Practical Application of Affinities. Tuesday and Thursday mornings we have chores."

"Laundry, dusting, vacuuming, polishing," Camilla said. "Real fun. There's grounds work too. Pruning, mowing, weeding. Leaf raking in the fall. Ugh, fall's the worst."

"And afternoons are for trying to access the garden," Julius said. "'Garden duty,' Mrs. Peavey calls it."

"We've tried everything," Camilla added. "I've manipulated the statues to match the versions Julius sees through his spyglass. Kenji has teleported from the patio onto every square inch of the garden, hoping to trigger a doorway. Julius

has walked the place, looking for hints with his spyglass. We've tried all this stuff together, individually, in different orders, and *nothing happens*."

Julius said, "Four magi and we're completely useless."

Piper paused. "There's only three of you."

The room grew quiet. Julius and Camilla exchanged worried glances.

"There *were* four of us," Kenji squeaked out. Julius glared. "What? She was gonna find out eventually."

"What's going on?" Piper demanded.

Julius bit his bottom lip but nodded at Kenji.

"Theodore Leblanc," the boy announced. "His affinity was time bending, he was my best friend, and he's been missing for ten days."

"What happened to him?" Piper asked.

Julius shrugged. "No one knows. I was the last person to see him. The night before he disappeared, he told me he thought he'd figured out a way into the garden. The next morning he was gone. Never showed up for breakfast. Never showed up for anything again."

"So he found a way in?"

"Maybe. I think he got in and then got trapped there—or worse."

"I think he was full of it and he's just off with Mrs. Mallory," offered Camilla.

"I think he found the way in and told Mrs. Peavey

and Mrs. Mallory, and then they killed him," Kenji said dramatically.

"Don't be ridiculous," Julius snapped. "They *want* us to get into the garden. Why would they kill him for figuring it out?"

"'Cause they thought they could get in too, doing whatever he did," Kenji said. "But they couldn't. It didn't work for them. 'Cause only a kid can enter the hidden garden." He said this last part very theatrically, eyes practically flashing as they locked with Piper's.

"Kenji has this theory that adults can't unlock the garden," Julius said with an eye roll. "That only an 'innocent, uncorrupted' child can get in." He put air quotes around *innocent* and *uncorrupted*.

"Kenji, you are the least innocent person I know." Camilla flung a finger at him. "You made us all ice cream cones filled with mayo on April Fool's. You're evil."

"Just think about it," Kenji countered, waving Camilla off. "Why else would Mrs. Mallory spend all this time teaching us how to use our affinities?"

"To help her get the elixir just as the current members of the High Order of Magi asked her to," Julius said. "We know this already."

"Sure, but Mrs. Peavey has never spent a day with her own daughter"—Kenji glanced at Piper—"and we're supposed to keep believing that she'll adopt us if we succeed?" He shook his head. "Plus, Mallory and Peavey are more powerful than us. They've been magi for far longer. The truth is they can't get into the garden, period. Not even if they know how. They *need* us to do it."

"Then why would they have killed Teddy?" Camilla said, exasperated.

"Well, they didn't know how much they truly needed him until after they . . ." Kenji stuck his tongue out and drew a finger across his neck.

Camilla made a gagging noise. "You've watched too many horror movies, Kenji. I'm sure Teddy is fine. Mrs. Mallory probably took him on her errand and forgot to tell everyone."

"A time-bending errand?" Kenji asked skeptically.

"Yeah. Why not?"

"Because Teddy disappeared two days before Mrs. Mallory left!"

"Mrs. Peavey said she was looking into it," Julius interjected. "We just have to wait and be patient."

"I don't trust anything she says right now," Kenji said. "She's not herself. Something's up."

"I'm telling you: Teddy got into the garden and something happened to him in there," Julius concluded matter-of-factly. "It explains why Mrs. Peavey can't find him. And Mrs. Mallory always said there would be tests once you got inside, puzzles or enchantments that you'd have to beat to get to the elixir. Teddy probably didn't beat them. Which is exactly why

we need to keep working together, just like we promised we would. Any progress gets shared with the group immediately. If we find a way in, we go in *together*. We tackle any test *together*. Then we all get adopted. That's what we agreed on. What happened to Teddy might be his own fault—especially if he moved forward without us."

Camilla nodded adamantly, but Kenji fiddled with his jacket's cuff. This was his best friend who was missing.

"So, Piper, what do you think?" Julius asked. "Are you with us?"

But all Piper could think about was what this whole thing meant: Magi were real. Affinities were real. Teddy had likely accessed the garden—the real, live version she'd seen in Julius's spyglass—and if this magical version of the garden was real, it meant the elixir of immortality was real too.

Hidden somewhere on the grounds of Mallory Estate, there was a drink that could save her father.

Chapter Eight

The Shimmering Doorway

That evening Piper found herself back in the kitchen, but this time, she got to see the children at work. Julius chopped and measured ingredients while Kenji worked diligently at the stovetop, keeping pots boiling or simmering at precisely the right levels. Everyone had a task, and for Piper, it was peeling carrots. All the while, Camilla ping-ponged around the kitchen, sampling sauces and stirring pots as she shouted out instructions. It was organized chaos.

The children ate when they could, shoveling down each course in the kitchen while Sophia dined on hers in the other room. When Sophia was done eating, she discarded her napkin and left without so much as a thank-you. Did she know that Piper was back here in the kitchen with the other children, falling in line and following orders? Did she even care?

"Wait! Magi Studies!" Piper shouted as she burst into the hall and ran after her mother.

"I'm sorry?" Sophia asked, turning to face her.

"Studies, training, whatever you call it. There's a class tomorrow, right?"

"Concealment Studies is on Wednesdays, yes," her mother confirmed.

"Where do you meet? What time? I want to come."

"Do you have an affinity?"

"Well, no."

"Then it would be a waste of my time, training a hollow," Sophia said. "Don't you agree?"

"But—I just—Julius said . . ."

It was no use. Sophia was already walking away, the Persian sauntering just a few steps behind.

Piper stormed back to the kitchen, fuming. "She is the *worst*!"

Julius looked up from where he was washing dishes, and Kenji teleported into view with another stack of dirty plates. Camilla flung a towel at Piper so she could help dry.

"She won't let me study with you guys," Piper explained. "Not unless I have an affinity. And I know you insist I have one, Julius, but it hasn't presented itself in twelve years, so I doubt it's going to anytime soon."

"Maybe you can find your affinity on your own," Kenji offered.

"It's still crappy that your mom won't help," Camilla said. "Mrs. Mallory helped Julius pinpoint his—and she helped *all* of us strengthen our affinities, even if we already knew it when we arrived. Since Mrs. Mallory's not here, those jobs should fall to your mom."

Piper wasn't sure where this small dose of kindness was coming from, but she appreciated it.

"I can try to help," Julius said. "I remember the bulk of what Mrs. Mallory said when we . . ." He froze.

The Persian had backtracked to the kitchen and was sitting near the fridge. Its head was cocked to the side, an ear turned deliberately toward the conversation. It noticed the kids watching and blinked calmly, then turned its attention to cleaning its paws.

"Let's talk about this later," Julius suggested. Even as he said it, it seemed silly. It was just a cat. But Piper found the hairs on the back of her neck rising.

"Yeah, sure," she agreed, eyeing the cat suspiciously.

They finished the rest of the dishes in silence.

When the sun had set and the stars had begun emerging, Piper slid from her bed. She tiptoed to the door, cracked it open, and peered into the hall. The Persian was waiting near the landing. Its ear perked up; Piper closed the door before the animal could whip its head around and find her.

She paced the room, panicked. What the heck was she

going to do? How was she supposed to talk to Julius if the cat was always shadowing her? She picked up her phone again, praying for service even when she knew she wouldn't find it.

How was her father doing? Was Aunt Eva trying to send updates? No, it wasn't the weekend yet, but even then, would Piper receive them? She'd never thought she'd want to see her grandmother so badly.

Piper came to a standstill before the balcony. To her left, the bookshelf remained mostly empty, save for the few books Piper had unpacked from her duffel and set on the shelves. Beside the bookshelf was a door.

Piper frowned at it. She hadn't noticed this before. The trim was painted the same pale blue shade as the wall, and the doorknob hardware also seemed to have been picked to be overlooked.

Julius's room was next to hers, Piper realized. On the other side of this door.

She made a fist and knocked softly, just in case the Persian was listening.

The door cracked open. Julius's face peered through.

"The Persian was in the hall," Piper whispered. "And it's past curfew. I thought it might get my mom if I—"

Julius grabbed her wrist and hauled her into his room. It was identical to hers in layout, only it looked lived-in. Clothes were scattered over the floor, and several dresser

drawers yawned open. The bookshelf was stocked full with reading material.

"No, that's smart," Julius whispered back. It seemed to go without saying that whispering was the only way to discuss things past curfew. "You should always use the shared door at night. Just knock first. For obvious reasons."

Piper blushed at the realization that her room was connected to a boy's and either of them could barge into the other's room at any moment, unannounced. "But I did knock," she managed to say.

"Yeah, and I'm grateful for it. Teddy was always forgetting." Julius's face fell. "He used to have your room."

"Oh," Piper said. She wasn't sure how she felt about living in the room of a possibly dead and most definitely missing boy. "What happened to all his things?"

"Your mother boxed everything up."

Because Teddy was gone and wouldn't be coming back? Or because her mother was behind his disappearance and wanted to bury any evidence of him as quickly as possible? Both were awful to think about.

"So earlier, in the kitchen," Piper began. "How did my grandma help you find your affinity?"

"You need to make a list of anomalies you've experienced," Julius explained. "Things that looked funny. Events that felt unnatural. Moments of déjà vu. That's what Mrs. Mallory had me do when I first arrived. A friend of hers helped place

me here when he realized I was a magi. I'd been bouncing between foster homes, mostly around Waterbury, and him spotting my aura was the best thing; Mrs. Mallory looked at my list and pinpointed my affinity on the second guess. From there, we picked out an amplifier."

Piper thought again about that odd day at the aquarium, and how her classmates often didn't acknowledge her, and how the hospital staff always avoided eye contact. How even her own mother had seemed surprised by Piper's presence that day they played peekaboo in her closet.

Feeling somewhat silly, Piper shared these moments with Julius, leaving out only the hospital because she didn't want to get into that with him yet.

"The aquarium is self-explanatory," he said when she finished.

"It is?"

"Yes, the men were magi hunters. Their binoculars were probably like my spyglass, an amplifier of sight. Mrs. Mallory says there are bad magi out there who are desperate to find hidden artifacts like the elixir of immortality, and they'll pay hunters to bring them magi children. Children who might be able to help them locate magi artifacts."

"And by 'bring' you mean ... kidnap?" Piper said in shock.

Julius nodded. "Most magi only have one affinity. So if a hunter is after a certain artifact and needs a certain affinity to reach it, a kid with the matching affinity is the perfect

solution. The hunter gets their prize and they don't have to share it with anyone. It's just another reason we're lucky to be here at Mallory Estate. Foster children with a shot at adoption, not kidnapped prisoners of some crazed artifact hunter."

Piper turned this piece of information over. "So what about my other anomalies?"

The boy rubbed his chin for a moment. "How did you feel in those moments?"

"Overwhelmed," Piper answered. "Nervous or anxious. Like at school . . . When I was tardy, I was scared to get lectured in front of everyone. At lunch I was embarrassed no one wanted to sit with me anymore. I used to have Bridget, but even she's bailed—says I'm always either angry or sad lately; that I'm no fun to be around."

"Hmm . . ." Julius thumbed his lip.

"Granted, I feel overwhelmed here, too, and nothing strange has happened. I'm probably a hollow. It was silly to think otherwise."

"Piper, you saw the garden—the *real* garden—through my spyglass. You wouldn't be able to do that if you were a hollow. We'll figure out your affinity, and then you can train and study with us."

She nodded weakly. "Can I see it again—your spyglass?"

He plucked the amplifier from his nightstand and they stepped onto his balcony together.

It was a cool summer night, the moon high overhead.

Fireflies danced near the tennis courts and carriage house, but they seemed to avoid the garden, as if they knew better than to venture there. Julius handed over the spyglass and Piper looked through the eyepiece.

The live version of the garden appeared for her, but instead of feeling shocked as she had the first time she saw it, she felt . . . inspired. Like she was witnessing some beautiful secret. She believed Julius now—believed all of them. This was *real*.

At night, the garden's trees glowed and twinkled, their trunks and limbs woven with strings of white light. It was like a winter wonderland, without the snow.

Piper scanned the head of the butterfly, where the Persian had been pacing the other day. The pedestal at the center of the pool held a metal sculpture shaped like an infinity symbol. Piper's heart kicked in her chest. Her locket seemed to warm against her skin.

An infinity symbol.

An elixir of immortality.

She continued to search the garden, following the paths, examining the various pools, not entirely sure what she was looking for. An entrance? It wouldn't reveal itself to her randomly when Julius had been looking at this version of the garden for years.

"If Teddy was stuck in the garden, wouldn't you see him with this?" she asked.

Julius shook his head. "The spyglass lets me see the truth before magi involvement, so basically: what this place looked like before the garden was concealed. A snapshot in time. If I want to see what's actively happening in the hidden version right this second, I'd need to be a *lot* more powerful."

The two stag statues at the edge of the patio came into view, and Piper froze.

Hovering above the right-hand stag at the garden's entrance, perfectly centered between the beast's antlers, was a shimmering disk of light. White and pearlescent, it rippled at the edges, like the surface of a pond being disturbed.

"Do you see that?" she said, passing the spyglass to Julius and pointing. "Above the stag statue."

He brought the amplifier to his eye. "See what?"

"There's something rippling there. It's white. Round."

"I don't see anything."

She snatched the spyglass back and looked again. The pocket of shimmering light remained, clearer than ever. Why was she seeing it tonight, when she hadn't yesterday? Maybe because she now believed; she'd accepted the secret of Mallory Estate.

"Huh," Piper heard herself saying. "It's gone. Must have been a trick of the light."

It wasn't that she didn't trust Julius. But she knew what would happen if she was honest. He'd call a meeting, tell the

others, and the children would all inspect the shimmering disk together.

Piper said good night to Julius and slipped back to her room using the shared door. As she lay in bed—head resting on the pillow Theodore Leblanc had once used and staring up at a canopy that he'd once stared at—she wondered if she was following in his footsteps.

If he'd found that same shimmering pocket.

If, when she crawled through it tomorrow, she might not live to tell the tale.

She should have been scared, but she was brimming with excitement. With hope. If the elixir was real, it would change everything. If the elixir was real, it meant her father could come home. And Piper would see that happen, even if it meant denying the others the adoption they craved.

Chapter Nine

Into the Garden

When morning broke, Piper was no longer upset about being barred from Concealment Studies. In fact, not being allowed to join the class suddenly looked like a happy turn of events. When everyone was busy learning, she'd have the garden to herself.

She snuck downstairs, grateful to be the only person awake. Not even bothering with breakfast, she headed straight for the patio and paused before the headless stags that marked the entrance. Their gold finish was dull and cracking, nothing like the pristine statues she'd seen through Julius's spyglass.

Piper had brought nothing with her for this excursion but the clothes she was wearing—her Yankees cap, a pair of jean shorts, and a tee from a 5K she'd run with Aunt Eva last

summer to raise money for cancer research. Now, staring at the statues, she was wondering if she should have brought a compass or her notebook or at the very least some rope. How was she going to get through the shimmering pocket? When she'd looked through the spyglass, she could envision herself scrambling up the right-hand stag's back, climbing his neck, and holding on to his antlers as she launched herself through. But the statue was headless; there weren't any antlers to use for balance. And despite the fact that the stag was lounging, it was still quite large; its back was well above Piper's hip, its neck level with her head.

A mourning dove cooed in the distance, and Piper scrambled up the stag. Everyone would be waking soon, and the day's lessons wouldn't keep the kids from breakfast. The kitchen was dangerously close to the patio. She had to be fast.

Piper made it up the stag easily enough—all those years of gymnastics had paid off—and soon she was standing atop the severed head as though it were merely a tree stump. This would be the tricky part. She tried to imagine where the antlers would be, eyeballed where she'd seen the shimmering disk the night before.

If she dove forward, sort of like a dive off a diving board, she could pass through the disk and land in the garden below. But there was the trouble of the landing itself. She'd need to get her feet beneath her before hitting the ground.

A front flip would do the trick, and the height of the stag

statue meant she should have enough time to execute it.

Before she could lose her nerve, Piper jumped—up and forward—then tucked into a flip.

Her landing was sloppy, and she pitched forward, throwing a hand out to stop herself from face-planting. The grass beneath her fingers was *green*. She straightened slowly, and her mouth fell open. The oak alley stretched before her, a canopy of lush leaves casting the path in shadow. Alive, the trees seemed twice as large, twice as regal.

She'd done it. She was in the garden. The hidden one.

She glanced back at Mallory Estate. *It* was what looked dead now—gray and deteriorating. The ivy climbing the facade was brittle. The bricks, crumbling. Several of the windows were cracked and the patio was devoid of furniture. The place looked like it had sat empty for years. Above the statue she'd used to enter the garden, just between the stag's antlers, she could make out the shimmering portal that would bring her back. For some reason she could see it now, in this version of the garden. Peering within its perimeter, she could make out the real version of the estate: clean, definitely not crumbling. She'd be able to climb the stag and scramble back through the shimmering doorway to return to it later.

She thought of Julius and the others, likely waking in the other version of Mallory Estate right now. Would they come looking for her when she didn't appear at breakfast, or would they head straight to their studies with her mother and not

think much of Piper's absence until the lesson concluded?

She was too excited to dwell on it. There was no Persian to bother her here, no chance of running into her mother. She had the garden completely to herself—unless she ran into Teddy.

"Hello?" Piper called.

Birds chirped from the trees. A dove cooed again in the distance.

"Hello? Teddy?"

Still nothing.

Piper stuffed her hands in her pockets and started up the oak alley. Garden beds wrapped around the tree trunks, daffodils and roses and marigolds blanketing the floor in color. The path continued beyond the oak alley, and Piper stayed on it, following it into the center of the butterfly, where multiple pathways converged. Here, two long, narrow pools sat on either side of the central path. She'd seen these yesterday, but they were active now, their fountain spouts spraying mist into the air. And the statues atop each pedestal were pristine, gleaming, not a speck of discoloration on their golden finish.

Piper continued, walking in a bit of a trance, until she reached the pool that held the infinity statue. Sunlight bounced off the crystalline water and danced over the sculpture. Like the women in the mirrored pools, the infinity symbol was perched atop a pedestal, and it spun idly in the breeze, rotating like a weather vane. It was actually a metal ring, she realized, warped and imperfect. It only looked like an infinity symbol when it twisted just so, when viewed from a certain angle. It was as if the sculpture had a secret, like it was trying to hide the truth.

Piper stepped nearer, heart pounding in her chest.

Positioned along the edge of the pedestal and curling down into the water were *steps*. A staircase. Leading into the pool. And there, at the bottom, set into the stone base, was a wooden door with a metal latch.

This felt too easy.

The pool wasn't that deep. Maybe ten, twelve feet; no worse than the deep end of a swimming pool. Piper could hold her breath and swim down. How she'd get the door open against the water she had no idea. Maybe there was a way to drain the pool, a lever she couldn't see.

She'd search as she swam.

Piper ditched her cap, kicked off her shoes and socks, and stepped onto the bricks that made up the border of the pool. She took a deep breath.

But just before she jumped, a voice said, "I wouldn't do that."

Piper yelped and her foot slipped out toward the water. Someone grabbed her wrist and yanked her to safety.

It was a boy. A boy a few years younger than her—roughly Kenji's age—with brown hair, blue eyes, and fair skin

that had reddened with sunburn across his cheeks and limbs. He was wearing a Red Sox T-shirt and a pair of green cargo shorts that held a water bottle in one pocket, and he was squinting at her as though *she* were the one who'd appeared out of nowhere.

"You're Theodore Leblanc," Piper murmured.

"Yeah. Teddy. And *you* must be new." He glanced at her baseball cap in the dirt, eyes narrowing. "When did they bring you in?"

Piper blinked, speechless.

"Peavey and Mallory," he clarified. "When did they bring you to the estate?"

"Two days ago," she managed.

"And you already found your way in? Wow. I'm impressed. What's your affinity?"

"You're supposed to be dead."

"Sorry to disappoint you." Teddy stretched his arms wide, making a show of himself. "Not dead. Very much alive, actually, and kinda concerned why anyone back home thinks otherwise."

He blinked at Piper, clearly waiting for an explanation, but she was still staring between him and the pool. "I'm sorry," she said, waving a hand at the water, "but why can't I go in?"

The boy walked to the outer edge of the dirt path, where flowers grew, and plucked a pansy free. Then he tossed it into

the water. Instead of floating, the flower sank like an anchor, swift and straight. Piper thought she even heard a muted thud as it hit the stone bottom.

"It's cursed. Protected. Whatever you want to call it," the boy said. "I figured it out by accident. Was about to dive in myself when a bee landed on the surface and got sucked straight down to the bottom. From what I can figure, you have to do them in order."

"Do what in order?"

"The trials. There's three of them, and then the infinity pool drains and you can reach the elixir. I mean, at least I'm assuming that's what's beneath that trapdoor. The statue is kind of a giveaway." He glanced toward the estate. "I told Mrs. Peavey all this. Didn't she send you in with the first key?"

"What key?"

"The key for the first trial," Teddy said, clearly getting frustrated. "I told Mrs. Peavey where to find it when I told her that I'd figured out how to get into the garden. I wanted to tell everyone, but she said she didn't trust Mrs. Mallory and that we should keep things quiet. She told me to lie low for a while, stay hidden inside the garden. She *promised* she'd retrieve the key and send you guys in with it when it was safe."

"I don't know anything about a key," Piper admitted, trying to keep up.

Color drained from Teddy's face. "Did she at least say I could come home with you? I'm tired of hiding—*and* I'm running low on food."

Piper was struggling to follow. "Can't you just leave through the doorway?"

"What doorway? I used my amplifier to get in here." He reached into his pocket and withdrew a golden pocket watch with a dragonfly etched into the back. "I first discovered a way into the garden by bending time. I hid on the patio and went back to the very moment when the High Order of Magi created three trials to guard the elixir and hid the garden. I saw them bury the first trial key too, beneath the carriage house. But I didn't go in then. I returned to the present and told Mrs. Peavey everything I'd discovered. I was going to tell the others, but Mrs. Peavey told me to hide in the garden—immediately—otherwise Mrs. Mallory would kill me and absorb my affinity so she could get in the garden herself. So I bent time again and slipped into the garden just before the magi concealed it. Mrs. Peavey said she'd send you guys in—with the key—so I've been waiting."

"I'm sorry, but I don't know what you're talking about, Teddy," Piper said. "None of the kids are sure where you are. Julius didn't mention any key. He thinks you died trying to complete a trial in here. Camilla says you're off helping Mrs. Mallory on an errand. Kenji has this crazy theory you were murdered."

"Mrs. Peavey should have updated you all," Teddy said, shaking his head. "I don't understand."

But Piper did. At least, she was beginning to suspect she might. "Teddy," she said quietly, "I think she tricked you. I think she meant to trap you in here."

And that was when Theodore Leblanc fainted.

Chapter Ten

The Trapped Boy

I didn't faint," he argued. "I just needed to sit down for a second."

Piper didn't point out that sitting would have involved Teddy's head staying out of the dirt; there were more pressing things to discuss.

"She wouldn't have trapped me," he insisted, leaning forward to rest his sunburnt arms on his knees. "She seemed scared when she told me to hide. *Terrified*. She said Mrs. Mallory couldn't be trusted. No way she's that good of an actor. And also"—his gaze drifted toward her cap, eyes narrowing—"I really don't think I should trust someone who wears Yankees paraphernalia."

Piper rolled her eyes. "Spoken like a true Sox fan." She picked up her cap, put it back on, and crouched beside him.

"Teddy, my grandmother has been missing since I got here. None of the kids have seen her in over a week. If my mom wasn't lying to you—if she was scared of my grandma for some reason—she's had plenty of time to update everyone. But they have no clue where you are."

"Hang on, back up. Your mother and grandmother?" Teddy's eyes bulged.

"Yeah. I'm Piper Peavey. Sophia's my mom. Melena's my grandmother."

"Huh," Teddy said. "I didn't know Mrs. Peavey even had a kid."

That sounded about right. Fostering children? Totally cool. Mentioning your biological flesh and blood to those kids? Not in a million years.

Teddy brushed a bit of dirt from his knee and glanced toward Mallory Estate. "There must be something else going on. Mrs. Peavey wasn't lying. Maybe she didn't update you fully."

"Teddy, no one knows how to get into the garden but you. You're the only one who figured out how to access it, and none of the other kids have an affinity for time bending. So my mom was *clearly* lying when she said she'd send us to help you."

"Oh." Teddy looked suddenly embarrassed. "I guess I didn't think of that."

"Don't take it too hard. Sox fans aren't particularly bright."

His features hardened. "It was a very stressful moment, okay? Your mom had just told me that Mrs. Mallory would kill me and absorb my affinity so she could get the elixir herself! Of course I hid. I trust her, okay?"

"Maybe you shouldn't," Piper muttered, then added, "And my grandma wouldn't hurt a fly."

"Just forget it. We'll talk to your mom, and she'll explain everything. You'll see. Now, how *did* you get in here?"

"I saw a doorway—a glimmering pocket of light—with Julius's spyglass."

"So your affinity is sight also?"

"Beats me." Piper shrugged. "Despite what Julius keeps insisting, I'm not convinced I have an affinity. And to be perfectly honest, I didn't believe in any of this"—she made a sweeping motion at the garden—"until yesterday morning."

"But you still found an entrance that Julius couldn't see. Impressive." Teddy pushed to his feet. "Well, no use wasting any more time. Let's go talk to your mom and get that key— it's buried beneath the carriage house."

"No way! My mom purposely trapped you in here and has kept the key secret from everyone. My grandma's missing, and for all we know, that's her doing too. I don't trust her one bit."

Teddy's face scrunched up. "But she protected me from your grandma."

"My grandma's looking like a victim too!" Piper said breathlessly. How could he still be making excuses for her

mother? "Look, you stay here. *I'll* get the key. And if my mom's already gotten her hands on it—which I bet she has because she's clearly up to something—I'll find it and bring it back. Then you and I can get the elixir together before she makes anyone else disappear."

"Are you always this bossy?" Teddy asked.

"Are you always so clueless?" she countered. "How did you even survive out here all this time? And if you accessed the garden back when the High Order of Magi first hid it, how the heck am I even talking to you? *I* didn't go back in time to get in here."

Teddy shook his pocket watch at Piper. "I brought myself back to the present as soon as I was inside. That way any of the kids could bump into me when they came in with the key. As for food and stuff . . . Mrs. Peavey sounded *really* scared when she told me to hide. So, I don't know, something about that made me pack a bunch of supplies. I've been rationing, and refilling water bottles when it rains. I'm starting to run low, though, and I'm not gonna lie: I've considered bending time back to just before the concealment, sneaking out, and staying in the past—where I could easily get food . . . and a shower. But then how would you guys ever find me? How would Mrs. Peavey tell me it was safe to come home?" He slid his amplifier back into his pocket. "Doesn't matter. You're here now; everything's going to be fine."

Piper eyed his hair, noticing for the first time how greasy it was. There was also a thinness to him that she suspected wasn't his natural frame. Her mother was truly evil to have trapped this poor ten-year-old in the garden.

"Okay, so not so clueless," she admitted. "Just overly trusting."

Teddy forced a smile. "I'd rather trust people than assume everyone's out to get me."

But life *was* out to get everyone. As Piper's aunt liked to say, *Life is 100 percent fatal.* And with a mother as neglectful and selfish as her own, Piper had never been one to trust others blindly.

"I'll get the key," she said, glancing back at the looming, dead version of the house. "And when I do, I'll come straight back here. I promise."

"Just make sure you bring food and water. Actually, bring some even if you don't find the key within a day. I don't know how long I can last without stuff. Oh, and a flashlight and sleeping bag for the night would be great too."

Piper nodded. "Absolutely."

"And you'll update the others, right? I was going to tell them I found a way in, I just ran into Mrs. Peavey first, and then, well, you know." He paused, biting his bottom lip. "I don't want them to think I broke our agreement."

Piper hesitated. If she involved the others, there was no way she'd be able to take the elixir to her father. Camilla had made it clear that the elixir was the kids' ticket to a permanent home. They'd give it directly to Sophia.

"I know you trust my mom, Teddy, but I don't," she said. "If I tell the others, it's bound to get back to her. They're all so eager to please her, to find the elixir, and I get why, but I just can't risk her knowing that I've met you. Not until I figure out why my mom trapped you in here—and what happened to my grandmother."

Teddy nodded slowly. "Okay. I'm cool with that for now. But we have to tell them eventually."

"When it's safe to, yes," Piper agreed.

They walked back toward the estate. Birds sang from the oaks. Sunlight filtered between the leaves.

"So what's your story, Teddy?"

"I lived in New Haven with my foster dad before coming here. He's a magi too. He helped me select an amplifier and was always having me take him back in time to try to save his wife. She died in a hit-and-run. We could never stay in the past long without messing up our futures, so I'd always bend us home, and he'd rush through the house, calling her name, hoping she'd be there."

Teddy rubbed the back of his neck. "He tried so many things when I'd bend time. Small changes on the day she died. One time, he even followed her around, waiting for the car to come swerving toward her, and pulled her out of the way. It didn't matter. Every time we'd come back to the

present to learn she'd died in a hit-and-run some time that same week. Like it was fated to happen.

"He started wanting to go farther back—a few days before her death, a week earlier, then to her childhood. But I was only seven at the time and that sort of bending was draining me like crazy. He got angry." Teddy rubbed his jaw and looked at his feet. There was more to this story, Piper could sense, but if he didn't want to share it, she wouldn't pry.

"I've only lived here a year, but I love Mallory Estate," Teddy said after a moment. "I met Kenji, and Julius, and Camilla. We get to study magi history and strengthen our skills—and gosh, have I improved since I started receiving proper training. Plus, I don't have to hide my affinity from hollows here. It's been great . . . at least until I learned that Mrs. Mallory was after me. Figures that this place was too good to be true."

"What about your birth parents?" Piper asked.

Teddy shrugged. "No idea. I barely remember them, but I think they were magi too, because I've always known about affinities. The state refuses to tell me what happened to them. I'm guessing it was pretty awful and they're trying to spare me, but I'm ten now. I can handle it."

Piper nodded, understanding all too well. The doctors were always trying to spare her. Aunt Eva, too. But she just wanted the truth, even if it was hard.

"Well, this is my exit," Piper announced as they reached the stag statues.

Teddy stared, incredulous.

"Can't you see the portal?" She pointed at the shimmering disk between the stag's antlers.

"I've had garden duty every day since I've been here. If there was a portal, I would know." Teddy sounded downright offended.

"Well, it's there," Piper said, and explained what it looked like. Teddy peered at the statue doubtfully. "It's probably just as well that you can't see it. You were trying to stay hidden."

"I guess," he said. "But why can you see it and I can't?"

"Maybe you need to see it with the spyglass first."

Teddy looked unconvinced. "Yeah, maybe."

Piper climbed the statue. It was awkward and difficult, but soon she was sitting on the nose of the stag, looking through the shimmering portal between the antlers. She could make out the patio, populated with furniture. Luckily no one was outside.

"Hey, Piper?"

She looked over her shoulder.

"I'm really glad to have met you. Even if you do root for the spawn of the devil." Teddy's eyes flicked to her cap.

Despite the insult, Piper felt herself smiling. "I'm glad to have met you, too, Theodore Leblanc. I'll be back as soon as I can." And with that, she passed through the shimmering doorway.

Chapter Eleven

Disappearing Act

Piper's feet had barely hit the patio when the entry hall's French doors opened and the children of Mallory Estate came spilling through, Julius in the lead. He pulled up, frowning when he saw her. "Where have you been all morning?"

Had she really been in the garden that long? Time must have gotten away from her.

"Just getting a head start," she said quickly, hoping they hadn't seen her coming through the portal.

"On garden duty?" Camilla's face scrunched up doubtfully. Today she was wearing a tank top that said A FORCE TO BE RECKONED WITH. "You don't even know your affinity yet."

"I was just trying to get familiar with the layout."

"See anything interesting?" Camilla asked. "Because we share everything."

"No. But I was thinking . . . maybe we're going about this wrong. Maybe there's something we need to find first. Like a key."

Julius arched a brow. "A key? Why a key? Are you not telling us something?"

"Yeah, friends don't keep secrets," Camilla added.

"I thought we weren't friends," Piper pointed out.

"We're not. I mean, we sure won't be if you're hiding something."

"Not hiding," Piper insisted. "Just trying to find a way into the garden like the rest of you. And I was thinking that when things are hidden, or locked away, you usually need to unlock them first."

"There's a gate on the garden's east wall," Kenji said. "It's not locked or anything, but there *is* a keyhole."

"Interesting." Julius pursed his lips.

Camilla snorted. "You really think *that's* the entrance?"

"It's something we haven't tried yet." Julius turned to Kenji. "Can you go check it out?"

With a nod and a flip of his collar, Kenji blinked from existence. Piper looked anywhere *but* at Camilla, who was glowering like a disapproving parent.

Kenji reappeared on the patio, causing Piper to flinch.

"Given the state of the keyhole, we're looking for something old."

Camilla rolled her eyes. "What a surprise."

"Teeth no more than an inch tall," Kenji continued. "Likely bronze or gold to match the gate's other hardware."

"You really think it's that simple?" Camilla said, now staring down Julius. "That the entire garden was hidden by magic but a boring old key will open it up?"

"Teddy would say it was worth looking into," Kenji muttered.

Piper felt a twinge of guilt. She knew it wasn't smart to admit she'd found Teddy—not yet at least—but as Kenji looked longingly at the garden, she wished she could tell him that his friend was okay.

"Kenji and Camilla," Julius said, "you guys start with the first floor inside. Piper and I will handle the grounds."

"I'll search the carriage house," Piper offered, and broke into a jog, feeling Camilla's eyes on her back. She didn't believe Piper. And for good reason. Piper knew she was sending them all on a wild-goose chase. Her mother had trapped Teddy inside the garden and had probably already dug up the key. But Piper continued to the carriage house anyway. She didn't have to search long to confirm Teddy's story.

Crawling beneath an antique car, she found a loose floorboard and lifted it. A small hole had been dug in the

dirt. It was empty. The key had already been claimed.

And chances were it was in a restricted area of Mallory Estate.

Piper spent the rest of the day formulating a plan, and by the evening, she was ready. She waited until everyone was likely asleep and then she waited a bit longer. When the clock on her nightstand read one a.m., she slid from bed and nudged the doors to her balcony open. The hinges were old and rusty, and they squeaked no matter how careful she was.

She froze on the threshold, waiting, listening. The night was humid, the air heavy on her skin, but nerves made her shiver. When she was certain no one had heard her—especially not the Persian—she stepped onto the balcony and turned her attention to the ivy that covered the house. It was thick, like a blanket of rope. Piper grabbed a fistful and tugged. Thankfully strong, too, rooted deep into the bricks. She started climbing before she could lose her courage.

Soon she was on the turret—where all the ivy seemed to lead—working her way around its curved form, toward a window just below the roofline. It was unlocked. She pushed it open, crawled through, and collapsed on an unfinished wood floor. Dust billowed around her, nearly causing her to sneeze.

Piper held her breath, letting her eyes adjust to the darkness.

She was in what appeared to be an attic. Boxes and crates littered the space. A settee and dresser were draped in pale sheets. A child's desk and chair were covered in dust. Across the way there was a hole in the floor, where a winding staircase descended to the lower levels of the turret. Piper could make out the steep steps in a floor-length mirror that was propped against the wall just beside the stairway.

This place would take hours to search. The turret was four floors tall, and it was possible her mother hadn't even brought the key up here. It could be down two levels, stowed safely in Sophia's bedroom, or even hidden in the office on the first floor. Piper considered the stairs.

No. She should start here. Do this methodically. If she couldn't find the key tonight, she could try the lower floors tomorrow. But where to start . . .

She moved to the desk. Painted white, it seemed to glow in the moonlight that cut through the open window. The left side had two standard legs, but the right was solid, made of a stack of three drawers. Piper tugged the first drawer open.

Inside was a framed black-and-white picture. She lifted it out, blowing dust from the glass. An image of her mother and grandmother stared back, only Sophia was roughly Piper's age, and her grandmother the age of Sophia now. The young Sophia was smiling, but much like Piper's father, the smile didn't reach her eyes. Melena M. Mallory stood behind her, a hand resting on the girl's shoulder.

Piper reached for the next thing in the drawer—a journal. She angled it toward the moonlight and opened it. *This journal belongs to Sophia Mallory*, read the first page. Piper flipped through, pausing to read a dog-eared entry.

Still no signs of my affinity. Mom is getting frustrated. She keeps saying that some magi don't find their affinity until nearly fifteen, but I can tell she's saying this more for herself than me. What do I care if I can't teleport or manipulate elements or bend time? Not a single person at school can either, and what's the point of having powers if you can never use them?

Mom says the world fears magi, that we have to keep our affinities secret from anyone who doesn't have their own. It seems not having an affinity would make life a whole lot easier.

Tomorrow we're trying hypnosis. She says that my affinity might reveal itself if I'm in a more relaxed mental state. Gag. I can't wait to get out of this place. It hasn't been the same since Dad died, and once I leave, I'm never coming back.

The entry date put Sophia at thirteen. There were plenty of pages left in the journal, but Sophia hadn't written anything else.

Piper frowned. This didn't match anything she knew. If

her mother couldn't wait to leave Mallory Estate, why had she abandoned Piper and returned here?

Piper reached blindly into the back of the drawer. It was crammed with brittle school papers and notes scribbled to classmates. The second drawer held a pencil case and an old yearbook.

This was pointless.

If Sophia had found and hidden the key, why would she put it in the attic? What Piper needed was to get into *Sophia's* room. Maybe she could sneak in during the children's Friday lesson . . . so long as the Persian didn't follow.

Overwhelmed, Piper sat in the chair that accompanied the desk—and promptly fell to the floor as the old legs cracked beneath her.

Dust billowed.

Piper froze solid, the noise of the crash echoing through the estate. For what felt like an hour, she held deathly still, too terrified to move.

And then, from below: a faint *mew*.

Trembling, Piper dove behind the desk. She peered around the solid stack of drawers and watched the mirror near the stairwell. A shadow moved in the glass. Then white fur. The Persian.

Piper pulled back, hiding from view, fist clenched around her locket. This was it. The Persian would find her and then her mother would arrive. Piper would disappear the way

Melena M. Mallory had. Teddy would be stuck in the garden forever.

Regret lanced Piper. She should have told the other kids what she'd accomplished in the garden. She shouldn't have kept anything secret.

The Persian meowed again, closer this time. Most definitely *in* the attic. Adult footsteps followed. Piper heard them transition from stairs to wooden floorboards. She could barely breathe.

The Persian's mewling grew louder. It was so close now, maybe just feet from the desk. Piper squeezed her locket harder, wanting nothing more than to sink into the floor.

The cat rounded the desk and stared at Piper. Its yellow eyes gleamed wickedly. It cocked its head, blinked.

And then, to Piper's astonishment, it yawned and turned away.

Sophia appeared next, wearing a bathrobe that hung open over silk pajamas, her hair piled loosely atop her head. She walked within an inch of the school desk, but her gaze never dipped toward Piper.

"You must have sensed a mouse," she said bitterly to the Persian, and nudged the cat with her foot. "Back to bed. It's too late for this nonsense."

The Persian hissed but turned toward the stairs.

When their shadows had disappeared from the attic and their footsteps had faded, Piper finally exhaled.

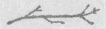

They hadn't seen her. It was as if she had vanished, as if she'd . . .

The ground seemed to shift as Piper made sense of what had happened.

All those times she'd felt ignored at school and at the hospital, how the fake security guards hadn't been able to find her in the pile of stuffed animals at the aquarium, the way her mother hadn't seen her playing peekaboo in the closet, and the way the Persian had overlooked her just now.

It was because she wasn't there. She really *had* disappeared.

Piper's affinity was invisibility, and she was pretty sure her locket was her amplifier.

Chapter Twelve

The Four Stags

I t had been a brisk October morning when Piper first put on the locket.

Atticus had thrown open one of the front windows of the bungalow and called out, "Get in here! I have something for you." Piper had abandoned the tire swing and skipped happily inside; "I have something for you" was code for "Want a present?"

Her father was sitting in the kitchen, the Sunday crossword spread across the table. He'd been perpetually sick for most of the summer, and he'd taken up the crossword as a hobby to fill the time he'd otherwise have spent at work, tearing down old apartment complexes across the state and building new ones in their place.

Atticus took a sip from his coffee and set the mug aside. "I

was cleaning out your mother's dresser," he began, and Piper immediately felt ill. She was nine then. Her mother had been gone for ages, and all that time Atticus had avoided her half of the master bedroom like it was the plague. A thick layer of dust coated the surface of the dresser, and the drawers hadn't been opened since Sophia last touched them. Piper wasn't sure if she should be glad her father was finally clearing out the room or concerned for the well-being of his lungs.

He gave a haggard cough, then slid the locket across the table. The silver chain was old and the locket itself was in need of a good buffing. "You should have this. I found it in your mom's jewelry box."

"But it's hers," Piper said uncertainly.

"Actually, it's yours. I bought the locket when you were born and put a picture of the three of us inside it. I was going to give it to you on your first birthday, even if you wouldn't have been ready to wear it for many years still, but by then, your mom was rarely around . . ." He pressed his lips together and swallowed, eyes glassy. "I could barely look at the locket after that, so I put it with her things, hoping she'd take it when she moved out. I never should have done that. It was a gift. Her picture inside, her leaving—none of that changes that I bought it for you."

Piper cracked open the locket. A foreign version of her family smiled up at her. Two parents, one baby.

"You can change the picture if you want," Atticus said.

"I like the picture," she admitted, and it was true. "Thanks, Dad."

"You want help putting it on?"

She nodded, and he fastened the clasp behind her neck. The locket hit her breastbone, cool and small.

"Does this mean I can't wear my Yankees cap anymore?"

Atticus grabbed it by the bill and gave it a playful shake, jiggling Piper's head. "Why would you ever think that?"

"I've seen the photo albums. Mom is so . . . fancy. She always wears jewelry, but never a baseball cap. I thought that maybe they don't go together."

"Eh, who cares? I say cap and locket are a perfect match." Atticus picked up his pencil and motioned at his puzzle. "Now, how about a little help on this crossword? I'm stuck on—"

"Ugh, Dad! Crosswords are so boring!" Piper sprinted for the tire swing. Atticus laughed behind her, his chuckles turning into a coughing fit before she even left the porch.

The next month the diagnosis came in. Atticus's years of work tearing down old buildings had exposed him to dangerous asbestos fibers. The cancer was in his lungs.

Piper didn't take her locket off after that, except for when she showered.

She touched it again now, lying in bed as the morning's first light began to break over Mallory Estate. She barely remembered the trip back to her room from the turret last

night. She'd made it safely, though, then spent the entire evening thinking of the locket. First while staring at the canopy of the four-poster bed, then dreaming of it.

She had a theory now for why she'd been able to see the shimmering portal above the stag when Julius hadn't. His amplifier showed the true state of the garden—what had been hidden by the High Order of Magi. But maybe only a magi with an affinity for invisibility could see the invisible doorway that accessed it.

Piper squeezed the locket in her fist. She still couldn't quite believe that she was like the rest of them—like Julius and Camilla and Kenji and Teddy. Like her *mother*. Piper had an affinity. She could become *invisible*.

She scrambled from bed and dressed quickly.

It was a Thursday, and the kids would be cleaning the estate all morning. Piper might not have found the key, but Teddy still needed supplies, and she'd have to be quick if she wanted to gather them without running into the others. She had no idea where to find a sleeping bag, but she did find a flashlight in the closet. She tucked it in her backpack and stole to the kitchen, grabbing a bunch of food for Teddy. When her bag was bulging, she paused.

They had folded bedding in the laundry room just the other day. Maybe some sheets or blankets were still down there. It would be the next best thing to a sleeping bag.

Piper darted for the basement and tiptoed down the

stairs. Her shoulder brushed the rack of keys again, making them jingle.

Keys!

Piper inspected them. There were four different sets. She counted quickly, heart racing. Each ring held twelve keys. Except for one, which had *thirteen*.

Could it really be hiding in plain sight? Piper lifted the set of thirteen keys off the hook. She didn't have time to compare it to the other rings and figure out which key was different, or to overthink her decision; returning to the garden with these keys was better than returning empty-handed. She raced down the steps and retrieved a few bedsheets that still sat folded atop the dryer. Then, after stuffing everything into her backpack and swinging it onto her shoulders, she darted back upstairs and out to the patio.

When she reached the stag, she glanced back at the house. If someone looked out a window at the same moment she jumped through the portal, the entrance to the garden would be obvious.

Piper grabbed the locket through her shirt and willed herself invisible. Was it working? She had no idea. She didn't feel any different, and she could still see her hands and feet, but that was all true last night as well. Of course, the idea of being caught by the Persian had terrified her in the attic. Maybe her fear had somehow triggered her affinity.

With a shake of her head, Piper mounted the stag.

Everyone would be waking soon, and if she wasn't invisible, she was going to look very strange standing on a headless statue.

She sized up the invisible portal and jumped through.

"Finally," Teddy exclaimed. He was leaning against the first oak in the alley just ahead, ankles crossed.

"It's barely dawn."

"I get cranky when I don't have food. Sorry."

"I believe that's called 'hangry.'"

"Hungry and angry. Yeah. Whatever. Did you bring anything?"

Piper handed over her backpack, which she'd stuffed with everything readily available in the kitchen: a box of cereal, a bunch of bananas, several water bottles, a few protein bars, and a container of leftovers from the previous night's meal: homemade mac and cheese. Camilla's specialty. Piper had never tasted anything so delicious.

Teddy pulled out the bedsheets she'd packed and practically drooled at the sight of the food. "Holy hallows, I love you. I haven't had this much to eat in . . . well, almost two weeks, I guess." He peeled open a banana and said through a mouthful, "Thanks."

"Sure, don't mention it."

He held the bag out toward her. "You want anything?"

"I had a banana already. Let's get to work." Piper fished

the keys from the bag and held them up for him to see.

"You found . . . a key ring," Teddy said skeptically.

"Well, I tried the attic turret first, but that was a bust."

Teddy's eyes bulged. "How'd you get up there?"

She told him about climbing the ivy and using her affinity to hide from the Persian. "Is it weird that I found my affinity on my own?"

Teddy shrugged. "Affinities are easiest to tap into in a moment of need. Adrenaline rush and all that. I'm sure there were already signs. I mean, I once made a twenty-minute quiz last almost an hour because I couldn't figure out one problem. I was bending time, only I didn't realize it, and I didn't even have my amplifier with me then. Adrenaline. Moment of need. Get it?"

Piper nodded. "But what about picking my own amplifier? Julius said my grandma helped him pick his."

"An amplifier can be almost anything, but it can help if the item has sentimental value, if it's something the magi has a unique bond with. Kenji's jacket was a gift from his mom before she died."

"And your pocket watch? Julius's spyglass?"

"They pair well with our affinities for time and sight. And since a locket has nothing to do with invisibility, I'm guessing that necklace is *really* special to you."

Piper touched it through her shirt. "Yeah," she said,

picturing her father, his cough, the crossword. Those final days before everything changed. "It is."

"Then it's not strange at all that you picked your own amplifier. Now, what's with the key ring?"

"I got lucky and brushed up against it this morning. This ring has a thirteenth key. The other sets only had twelve. And that got me thinking; maybe, just maybe, my mom might have hidden the key somewhere we wouldn't assume to look, where it's not really hidden."

She passed the keys to Teddy. He thumbed through them. "Smoking room, billiards room, patio doors, shed— *wait!* This is new." He paused on a dull steel key.

"It is?" Piper peered closer.

Something was stamped on the key's head. A butterfly. Like the knocker on the estate's front door. Like the design the paths made as they wove through the garden.

A flurry of excitement passed through Piper's chest.

"I know where this goes," Teddy said.

"Really?"

"There are a few statues on the outskirts of the garden." He grabbed a twig and drew the butterfly pathway in the dirt, boxed the insect inside a square, and then divided the entire thing into quadrants. Here and here"—he tapped the two top corners—"and two more down here." He touched the lower two quadrants.

"Four statues?" Piper said doubtfully.

"Each statue has a keyhole. And the statues share a theme, too. They're all stags."

"Like the two kneeling stags that guard the entrance," Piper murmured.

Teddy nodded. "I've had a *lot* of time to study the garden, and I say this is where we start. Turn the key in each of the statues and see what happens."

Piper didn't see any reason to argue. "Lead the way."

They went to the lower-right quadrant first, where a rearing stag of gleaming white stone stood atop a pedestal just beyond the outermost path. Behind it, Piper could see the rock wall that made up the eastern edge of the garden. Teddy brushed back the flowers at the pedestal's base, showing her a keyhole in the structure. The key slid into place and clicked audibly as Piper turned it.

The children stepped back, staring up at the stag. Nothing happened.

"Next statue, I guess," Teddy said, and retreated to the path that made up the butterfly's outer wing. They walked north.

Soon they were passing one of the rectangular fountain pools—the eastern one. The subjects of the three gold statues looked vaguely familiar, and Piper noticed a detail she hadn't the other day: one woman was weaving, the second was winding a length of thread, and the third held a pair of large shears.

"Are those supposed to be the Fates?" Piper said, pointing toward the statues.

"Yeah, I think so. They remind me of the Fates from Percy Jackson, just a lot younger."

"I love that series!" Piper had devoured all five of the Percy Jackson and the Olympians books over the course of Christmas vacation two years ago. The Fates in that series had been old and wrinkly, whereas these looked around her mother's age, but she couldn't deny that the statues beside her matched the Fates' roles of creating, measuring, and cutting the threads of life. A reminder of life and death felt fitting in a garden that held the key to immortality.

"The pool on the other side of the garden is exactly the same, butterflies being symmetrical and all," Teddy added.

"I saw it yesterday," Piper said.

They'd barely left the pool behind when he asked, "So why do you want it?"

"Huh?"

"The elixir."

"Well, we're supposed to find it, right?"

"Sure, but you already have parents, a home. Finding the elixir means getting adopted, and you don't need that. So why are you looking for it?"

She didn't like the way Teddy was peering at her. For a boy who trusted Sophia Peavey, it was a very untrusting look.

"I just want to help you all," she said finally.

"Let me get this straight. You don't want me to come back to the estate, and you're not telling the others you found a way into the garden either, but all this sneaking around solo doesn't mean you're in this for yourself?"

Piper stopped abruptly. "You know nothing about me, Teddy."

He eyed her cap. "I know you're a Yankees fan, and therefore untrustworthy."

She glowered at his Red Sox shirt. "I could say the same about you being a Sox fan. Also, you're here with me, aren't you? Last time I checked, two people can't do something solo."

He bit his lip, glanced at a clump of daffodils. "Just . . . this means a lot to us, Piper. Me and Kenji and the others."

"I know that."

"Good. Because there's a lot at stake."

"I get it."

"Okay."

"Okay." Sheesh. He was as bad as Camilla. "Is that the next stag?" She pointed to a statue over his shoulder. This stag stood proudly, head turned to the side as though it had just heard something in the distance. Its white stone body looked as smooth as glass.

"Yep. Stag number two." Teddy led the way off the path, then stooped beside the pedestal to pull back the flowers and show Piper the next keyhole. After fitting and turning the

key, they carried on in silence. Teddy seemed to sense she had no desire to talk anymore.

The third stag—head lowered while it grazed—was across the garden, in the third quadrant. And the fourth lay crumpled on its pedestal in the final quadrant of the garden, an arrow in its side. An archer stood over the dead animal, one boot resting on the prone stag's torso. Perhaps this was the noise the stag had heard two statues earlier: a hunter.

"Is every statue in here a reminder of death?" Piper asked.

Teddy shrugged. "Pretty much. The place looks nice when you first walk into it, but it's actually kinda creepy. I'm ready to leave." He gave her a long look. As much as Piper wanted to, she couldn't bring him out yet. At least not until she figured out what had happened to her grandmother and why Sophia had been keeping the other kids from Teddy.

Piper fitted the key in place and gave it a turn.

The archer moved, turning to face them. Piper yelped in surprise, toppling into Teddy, who promptly fell into the flower bed. Certain she'd imagined the archer's movements, Piper looked up.

He was most definitely moving. Piper and Teddy froze in the flowers, limbs tangled, as the archer opened his mouth and recited:

> *"To live forever is quite a feat;*
> *A fate that only the worthy may greet.*

One of courage and strength unmatched,
Who can face the worst and emerge unscratched.
So through the oaks to face your fears
Travel to unlock your limitless years.
Darkness is trivial for those with guile.
The fearless alone will unlock the next trial."

The hunter turned, putting his boot back on the stag.

"I'm sorry, what?" Piper said. But the archer had already gone stiff, his body returning to stone.

"Get off me," Teddy huffed, pushing Piper. She tumbled aside and he scrambled to his feet, waving his arms at the archer. "Hello? Come back! What does that mean?"

"That we have to face our fears to unlock the next trial?" Piper offered, fiddling with her locket. "But face them . . . how?"

"The oaks," Teddy murmured. "Didn't he say something about the oaks?"

They looked at each other, then broke into a run, sprinting for the path. Teddy took the lead, and when they hit the center path of the butterfly, he stopped abruptly. Piper barreled into him and he gripped her wrist, pulling her nearer.

"What is that?" he whispered, pointing ahead.

Several inches above the ground, a portal hovered in the middle of the oak alley.

It was nothing like the entrance Piper had used to access the garden. This portal was inky black. Its edges oozed and dripped, like oil overflowing a can.

"It's another portal," she said, peering into the darkness. There was nothing to see.

"It looks like a black hole."

"I think we have to go through it," Piper said.

"Be my guest." Teddy waved a hand at the pulsing portal.

Piper walked briskly forward. A coldness emanated from within, like a kiss of icy air.

"Wait, Piper. I was just kidding. I think we should talk about this first. I think—"

Chapter Thirteen

A Date with Fear

Everything was black.

Looking down, Piper couldn't even see her own feet. She waited for her surroundings to materialize—for something, *anything*, to appear—but the world remained colorless. Had the portal not worked? Was she stuck in some sort of limbo? If she was, how would she get out? What if she was forced to float in this pocket of darkness for all eternity?

Her heart beat wildly between her ribs.

She turned in circles, searching, squinting.

Once, when she'd been about six, she'd wandered into the basement of the bungalow, looking for a plastic sled that Atticus had stored away for the season. Sure, it was spring, and winter was behind them, but Piper had wanted to sled

down the stairs. It was pouring rain, and stair sledding sounded like an excellent break from her boredom.

While she was searching for the sled, the house shook with a loud clap of thunder and then plunged into darkness. Piper couldn't see anything, not even her hands in front of her face. She staggered, bumping into a wall, cobwebs brushing her cheek. Something fell on her head, cool and slick, and that was when she started screaming.

When Atticus found her, she was curled up at the foot of a bookshelf, shaking uncontrollably. In the glow of his flashlight, she could see that the slick thing had only been a tarp. But she'd been terrified of the dark ever since.

Now, with endless darkness surrounding her, Piper felt the same helplessness she had that day in the basement. Only this time, her father wouldn't be there with a flashlight to find her. This time, she was alone.

It's not real, she reminded herself. *The portal knows your fears. It's just inside your head. It knows what scares you.*

But if Piper didn't have a flashlight, if she couldn't see *anything*, how was she supposed to beat this?

Her heart jackhammered and she shifted her focus to it, exhaling with purpose, trying to calm her frenzied pulse. She imagined herself in the bungalow basement, surrounded by familiar smells. It was dark only because the power had gone out. Her father would bring a flashlight soon. Her pulse slowed, her breath came easier. Soon the darkness didn't seem so black. It was fading. There was something up ahead—a murky brown. She moved toward it.

A wall.

And not just any wall, but a rock wall, pocked and uneven. She followed it with her hands as it curved overhead.

A cave.

Piper hated caves.

She blinked and was suddenly surrounded by water so deep, she was treading in it.

An underwater cave. Even worse.

Piper took a gulp of air and dove, feeling blindly for a way out. Walls, walls, and—there. A tunnel, though she couldn't tell how deep it went. She shot to the surface and breathed, mouth tilted toward the cave's ceiling.

What if the tunnel dead-ends? What if you don't have enough air to get out?

"This isn't real," she said aloud, then took a giant breath and dove again, this time entering the tunnel. Even using the walls to propel herself forward, it didn't take long for her lungs to begin to ache. But she could see light ahead now, crystalline blue. She ignored the burning sensation in her chest and swam on. Then she was out of the tunnel, sunlight filtering through the water.

She swam up, up, lungs screaming.

Piper burst through the surface and the water vanished. She was completely dry, standing in a blindingly white room.

After so much darkness, it stung her eyes, and she blinked rapidly. A machine beeped in the corner. A nurse stood near it, reading something.

Then she saw the bed.

"Dad!" She ran forward, grabbing his hand. He flinched in his sleep but didn't wake. The beeping behind Piper grew sporadic. It was a heart monitor, she realized. She could see the lines now, spiking and falling.

"It's time to say good-bye," the nurse told her.

"What? No. The doctors said this treatment would be the one to work. They said he might get better."

"I'm afraid that hasn't happened. It's time."

"Dad?" Piper shook his hand, tears building in her eyes. "Dad, wake up. I have to talk to you. Dad, please don't go."

Atticus Peavey did not stir.

"Dad!"

"You cannot keep him forever," the nurse said.

"You're supposed to come home, Dad. You can't leave." Piper flung herself on the bed, her cheek to his chest. She could hear his heartbeat, feeble and fleeting.

"Last chance. Say good-bye."

"No." Piper's lip trembled.

The machine released one long, endless beep before the room collapsed inward. Piper was tossed like laundry in a dryer, no sense of up or down, before she burst into sunlight and hit the dirt.

"Wow. You were only gone a second. What happened?" Teddy helped Piper sit. She was back in the garden, the oak branches stretching overhead. "Did you get the next key?" She could barely hear him. The long, drawn-out tone of the heart monitor still echoed in her ears, stealing her breath, making her gasp and retch. Tears streamed down her face. "Hey, what's wrong?" Teddy touched her shoulder. "Piper?"

"It's not real," she whispered, mostly to herself. "It wasn't real."

But it felt like it, and she hadn't been prepared. She couldn't lose him. She *wouldn't*. She had to get the elixir—before Sophia, before the other children, before anyone. She had to get the elixir because she had to save her father. He wasn't going to die. He couldn't leave her.

"Piper, you're scaring me," Teddy said, voice quavering slightly.

"I'm fine," she insisted, even though she wasn't. She wiped her cheeks, steeled her features. Not for Teddy's benefit—she couldn't care less if a girl crying in the middle of a dirt path made him uncomfortable. There was simply no way she'd beat this trial—get to the elixir—if she let her emotions take over.

"What did you have to face?" Teddy glanced toward the portal, which was still oozing and pulsing beneath the oaks.

"Darkness, an underwater cave, then my father in the hospital."

"Why's your father in the hospital?" Teddy asked.

For a moment she considered lying. If she told him, he'd know why she wanted the elixir. But she didn't have the energy, and she couldn't think of anything else that would reasonably have left her so distraught.

"Lung cancer," Piper explained.

"Oh, I'm sorry."

"People always say they're sorry. But you didn't cause it. You don't have to say that."

"I don't know *what* to say," Teddy admitted.

"Then just say that. Say, 'I don't know what to say.'"

"I don't know what to say," Teddy echoed weakly.

Piper nodded. "Thanks. How about you give it a try?" She jerked her head at the portal.

"Do I have to?" Teddy whimpered.

"Yes." This was the only way forward. Piper would try again too, just as soon as she got her heart rate under control.

Teddy let out a dramatic groan. "Ughhhhh, fine." He straightened and edged toward the portal. After sizing it up for a solid minute, he finally stepped through. Before Piper could enjoy the solitude, he came flying back.

"That was fast. Did you get the . . ." Piper noticed his empty hands and let the question die.

"My foster dad, earwigs, and clowns." Teddy shuddered. "I couldn't beat the clowns."

"They're just people dressed up in silly costumes and face paint."

"Exactly. Never trust someone who has to paint on a smile."

"I guess it just doesn't sound so scary."

"Yeah, well, what scares me doesn't scare you. Congratulations."

Teddy stalked off. Clearly she'd hit a nerve.

"Wait! That's it!" Piper shot to her feet. "What scares me doesn't scare you. So let's go in together."

"I am *not* going back in there," Teddy said firmly.

"We have to! This is the only way we get the next key. And maybe the portal won't show us clowns at all, because I'm not scared of them. It might look at us as one person."

"And what if it doesn't? What if it just gives us all our fears?"

Piper shuddered. She didn't want to face that hospital room again. "Then we can help each other through them."

Teddy chewed his bottom lip.

"We at least have to try," Piper insisted.

"I hate to admit it, but you're right." He held out his hand uncertainly. Piper took it and they stepped through the portal together.

It was dark again, but something was scuttling over Piper's feet. "Those are earwigs, aren't they?"

"Yep," said Teddy. "So glad we did this."

"How did you beat them last time?" Piper asked. She

could feel something squirming up her ankle now.

"I just ignored them and they finally went away. It's a lot harder to do when I can't see them and—holy hallows, they're crawling up my leg. AHHH!" Teddy let out the highest shriek Piper had ever heard and grabbed her hand.

"I can't feel my fingers," she complained.

"Piper, this was a terrible idea. Remind me to never forgive you. Ugh, they're up to my knees! How did you beat the darkness?"

"I just let my eyes adjust."

"I don't think I want to see earwigs all over me. I hate this, I hate this, I hate this."

"There," Piper said. The murky brown wall of the cave was coming into view again. "Move toward that wall."

"They're in my shoes," Teddy moaned.

"Just ignore them. Keep walking." She squeezed Teddy's hand. The bugs were squirming all over her legs now. She just had to keep moving. If they reached the cave, the critters would drown.

But when Piper's hand grazed the cave wall, the water never came. Light had overtaken the darkness, at least, and when she glanced at her feet, she was relieved to see that the earwigs had vanished.

"They're gone," Teddy gasped. He sounded both exhausted and relieved. "I swear I can still feel them, though."

"Yeah, me too," Piper admitted. "It's almost like—"

"AHHHHH!" Teddy's scream bounced off the walls. "There's a clown in the cave, there's a clown in the cave. PIPER, THIS WAS THE WORST IDEA EVER!" Teddy turned toward Piper, burying his face in her shoulder.

Standing in the corner of the cave was the most disturbing clown Piper had ever seen. He was smiling, but not in the friendly way circus clowns did. This was more of an *I want to eat you* way, and his teeth looked very sharp. He was also holding a bunch of red balloons.

"Okay, if that's how I always pictured clowns, I'd be terrified of them too," Piper confessed.

"A friend from school made me watch this horror movie about a clown. I think it traumatized me."

"I can see why."

The clown blinked at them and took a step closer. Then another. The red balloons bounced against the cave ceiling. He was only a foot away, then inches, then so close Piper clamped her eyes shut and grabbed the locket beneath her shirt.

There was a strange shift in the air, and a feeling of lightness passed over Piper. She cracked open an eye and found the clown turning in circles, dumbfounded, searching the cave.

Piper was invisible. Teddy, too. She'd used her invisibility to hide them both. She jerked her head toward the cave's tunnel, and Teddy shuffled for it, relinquishing his grip on

Piper's hand only when it became necessary to crawl.

Then they were spilling into a foreign room with unadorned dark green walls. A bed was pushed beneath the lone window, the blinds lowered.

The door burst open and a middle-aged man shot through. "You didn't save her!" he roared. "It didn't work. It *never* works. You're worthless!" He threw a glass in their direction and it shattered against the wall. Piper grabbed Teddy's hand and pulled him closer, shielding him behind her back.

"Where are you?" the man went on, turning around, his hands fisted. He threw open the closet, looked under the bed. "Get out here, you ungrateful brat! We're trying again. Right this instant."

Piper's affinity was still hiding them, she realized. This horrible man whom Teddy had lived with for *years* luckily couldn't see them. He turned in another circle, rubbed his bloodshot eyes, and then stormed from the room, shouting Teddy's name. As the door slammed in his wake, the room transformed, now white and sterile.

The hospital.

Piper trembled and her invisibility vanished.

"Time to say good-bye," the nurse said.

Piper shook her head, over and over, in small jerking motions, unable to tear her eyes from her father.

"You're not afraid of cancer," Teddy said slowly.

127

"Yes, I am."

"I mean, sure, as a result of this. But *this* fear"—he pointed at the bed—"you're afraid of losing your father." He glanced at the heart monitor, then back to the bed. "You have to make peace with it, accept that it might happen. That's how you beat this fear."

"That's stupid," Piper said. "Accepting this isn't going to beat it. It just means that I admit the cancer has total control over him. Over our family. Accepting this means the cancer will win, that the only outcome *is* losing him."

Teddy frowned. "Maybe it's a way to give you back a little power. If you say good-bye, it's a way to heal. Isn't acceptance one of the stages in the grieving process?"

It was. The final stage, according to Aunt Eva. But Piper didn't want to accept any of this. How could rolling over and surrendering allow her to *beat* cancer?

"It's time," the nurse urged.

"I can't." Piper shook her head. "I won't."

"I have an idea." Teddy drew his pocket watch from his pocket, flipped open the cover, and wound the top stem, sending the hands turning. Then he clicked the cover shut and squeezed the device between his palms. The nurse began to move backward through the room, gaining speed until she was leaving streaks of color in her wake. Piper's father sat up, shifted, rolled. IVs were removed. The number of tubes lessened. Then he was merely in a doctor's room, getting the

news. Then even the medical institutions faded and he was at home, in the bungalow, sitting at the kitchen table in his pajamas, reading the paper over a cup of coffee.

Time ground to a halt.

When Atticus spotted Piper, he lowered the paper and smiled. It was a real smile, the kind she remembered from before he got sick. It lit up his whole face.

"Dad!" She raced forward, crushing her cheek to his chest. His arms wrapped around her back and she breathed in, soaking in his warmth, the smell of dish soap on his hands. "I missed you."

She felt Atticus shift, opening his mouth to respond, but the world tilted and the room flattened, and Piper and Teddy were thrown back into the garden.

Lying between them in the dirt was a stubby golden key.

Chapter Fourteen

Invisibility Lessons

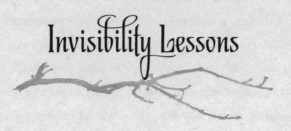

We did it," Piper breathed, watching as the fear portal collapsed in on itself and blinked from existence. She picked up the gold key. It was so small she could make a fist around it.

"Mmm, I don't know," Teddy said. "I'm not sure we truly beat all those fears. More like tricked some of them."

"Whatever, it worked."

"It did." Teddy nudged Piper with his elbow. "Thanks for helping me with the clown. Sorry I was so . . ."

"Rightfully terrified?" Piper offered.

Teddy laughed in relief. It was a beautiful sound, and for the briefest moment, the weight of her own fears from the portal lifted off her shoulders. "I thought maybe you'd make fun of me for all the screaming."

"No way. After seeing that clown, I think I'm afraid of them now too. So thanks for that. Also, your foster dad? He was *awful.*"

"Yeah. I was really grateful when Mrs. Mallory offered him money so she could take me."

That didn't sound at all legal or like any legitimate foster care operation, but Piper was starting to suspect that magi norms were very different from the rest of the world's.

"Did he . . . ?" she began, thinking of the glass he'd thrown in their direction, the way his hands had been curled into fists.

"I time-bent to avoid him, so he never actually got his hands on me. He'd always calm down eventually and apologize, then beg me to try to save his wife again. I time-bent in the portal, too, when I had to beat him solo. Your invisibility trick was a nice change."

Piper passed Teddy the gold key. "I think you should hold on to this."

He raised a brow. "Why?"

"Until I can trust my mom, I think it's safest with you. If she found me with that key . . ."

Teddy nodded. "Wanna tackle the next trial right now? I'm pretty sure I know where this itty-bitty thing goes, and . . ." He glanced at her cap, then grimaced, as though it pained him to admit what he said next: "It's nice when you're here. The garden gets lonely."

Piper fiddled with her locket. It was nice being with Teddy, too. He already knew all the progress she'd made in the garden because he was making it alongside her. And now he knew about her dad, also. There were no secrets to keep. Except maybe the fact that if they found the elixir, she wasn't about to hand it over to him so that he or the others could finally have their permanent home. If her father only needed a sip of the drink to get better, she could hand it over after. But who knew how many doses the bottle held. Atticus might need to drink the whole thing, and if that was the case, she'd let him.

An uneasy sensation pinched her side. She raised her chin, ignoring it. There was nothing to feel guilty about. Her father's life was at stake! She had to save him. And once she had, when all this was over, Piper would make sure that Atticus called the right people. Police, foster services. The children of Mallory Estate would get the homes they deserved. Everyone could win.

"It's getting late," she said, checking the sky. Garden duty had likely already started. "I'll come back as soon as I can. Hopefully tomorrow."

Teddy nodded, and he walked her to the patio, a comfortable silence between them.

"How did you do that?" a voice demanded.

Piper slid from the stag, freezing when her feet hit the

patio. Julius was sitting at one of the tables, a notebook laid open before him. Her heart pounded. He'd seen her reappear, blink into existence out of nothing.

If she'd been more cautious, she would have remembered to peer into the portal and search the patio before passing through. She'd have seen Julius sitting here.

She glanced over her shoulder, scanning the garden, but Camilla and Kenji were nowhere to be found.

"Did you give up the search for that key?" Piper asked Julius.

"No, Camilla and Kenji are still searching inside. I needed to think, so I came out here. Now, don't dodge my question. How did you do that?" Julius waggled a finger at her in a circular motion.

"Do what?"

"Appear out of thin air."

"Oh," Piper said, fiddling with her necklace. "I've been practicing."

Julius stared, confused.

"Invisibility," Piper said. "I'm pretty sure it's my affinity."

Julius gaped. "You figured it out on your own?"

"I ran into the Persian late last night, and he didn't see me."

Pure terror crossed Julius's features. "What were you doing out of bed?"

"Sleepwalking," she said quickly. "I came out of it in

133

the hall and the Persian was rounding the corner, and I just panicked. I knew I'd be in trouble for being out past curfew, and I stood there like a statue, wishing I could disappear—and it worked! The Persian looked down the hall—right through me—and walked away. I think my necklace is my amplifier. I had a death grip on it when it happened."

It was a fraction of the truth. She glanced at Julius, hoping he would buy it.

"How did he not smell you?"

"No idea," Piper admitted. "Maybe my invisibility shields me from all senses?"

"This. Is. Amazing!" Julius bolted out of his chair. "I've never met someone with an affinity for turning invisible. Can you show me?"

"Right now?"

"Yeah."

Piper touched her necklace and clenched her eyes. When she cracked an eye open, Julius was staring right at her. "Did it work?"

"No," he said flatly.

She tried again, concentrating so hard she began to sweat. She had no clue how she'd managed to disappear the other night or in the fear portal, and Julius was eyeing her like a teacher does before giving a student detention.

"You're still here," he said.

"Maybe I don't have the right amplifier," she added,

desperate for the conversation to be over before Julius could see through her lies.

"No, that's not it," he insisted. "An amplifier is just a tool, and it can be anything. Your affinity is inside you. It's *always* been there. You just have to tap into it. In a moment of need, it can be more easily summoned. . . ."

"Which explains last night with the Persian," Piper said. Adrenaline rush, just like Teddy had claimed.

"Exactly. But you need to learn how to summon your affinity in any instance, otherwise you'll never have full control over it." Julius rubbed his chin. "Mrs. Mallory always told us to picture our affinities as liquid energy. You are the well holding that energy. When you want to use it, you have to pull it from yourself and pour it into your amplifier. Once that power is in the real world, outside of you, it's easily accessible."

"That sounds really vague. And also kinda complicated."

"Just try it. Find the energy inside you and channel it into your amplifier."

Piper closed her eyes and immediately felt foolish. But she held her locket to her chest, rubbing the metal beneath her thumb. She focused on nothing but the feel of the necklace against her skin and the beating of her heart, and the world seemed to fall away. The twittering of birds faded.

She thought about the act of disappearing, of melting into nothing, and something twinged deep in her core.

Concentrating on this feeling, Piper envisioned a curling mist, water so lightweight that she could draw it from her, out of her, and into the locket. But she didn't stop there. She let the mist spread beyond the locket, enveloping her like a thick blanket.

"Piper! You're invisible!" Julius cheered.

"I am." It wasn't a question. Piper knew she was. She could feel the veil of her affinity around her, featherlight and warm, like a kiss of sunlight that shielded her from the world.

She opened her eyes. Julius was looking in her direction, but not *at* her.

"Go ahead and try dropping it," he said. "Let your amplifier empty."

Piper blew out a breath, and like a candle being extinguished, her affinity whooshed through the amplifier and back into her. Julius's eyes met Piper's.

"I can't believe you did it on your first try! Although maybe I shouldn't be surprised, knowing your bloodline."

"I wanna try again," Piper said, excited, but when she turned her attention inward, searching out her affinity, she felt . . . empty. No, *empty* wasn't exactly the right word. She could still sense her affinity pulsing inside her. It was more that the thought of summoning it felt impossible. It was distant, miles away, and she'd already run a marathon. There was no way she could summon even a drop of it.

"I know that look," Julius said. "You're drained. It's like a

well, remember? You have to let yourself refill."

"So, what? You can only use your affinity once a day?"

"No, but you have to keep practicing. Build up some endurance so that you're not drained every time you use it. It will get easier—*if* you keep training. You should come to Practical Application of Affinities tomorrow!"

Piper hesitated. Just yesterday, all she'd wanted was to be included in some official schooling, but now, time away from the garden seemed risky. Letting her mom know that she could become invisible didn't seem like the best idea either.

"Mrs. Mallory taught Friday class," Julius continued, "but we're carrying on without her while she's gone. I'm the teacher at the moment."

So Piper's mother wouldn't be there. Maybe she should train with the kids after all . . . so long as the Persian wasn't around. She didn't trust that white fur ball for a second.

"Okay," she agreed. "But don't tell my mother yet. I want to get really amazing at disappearing before I show her. Maybe she'll stop treating me like garbage if my skills are super impressive." *Also, I don't want her to know I can sneak around the estate invisible,* she added mentally.

"Your secret is safe with us," Julius said, and picked up his notebook. "Now let's check in on Camilla and Kenji. I left them in the library."

Chapter Fifteen

A Heart-to-Heart with Mom

The library was unreal. Glimpsing it through the French doors her first night at Mallory Estate hadn't done it justice. But now that Piper was inside, standing on the burgundy carpet, turning in circles to stare up at the towering stacks, she nearly lost her breath. There were enough books to keep a reader busy for a lifetime.

Gold curtains were drawn over the windows that faced the front drive, and a fireplace with a worn wooden mantel and stone facade marked one end of the room. Two upholstered chairs were angled toward the hearth. Flames in a library seemed like flirting with danger to Piper, but it was summer, and luckily, no fire was lit.

"Find anything?" Julius called out to Kenji. The boy was sitting at one of the workstations, reading a thick

leather-bound book beneath the glow of the desk lamp.

"Not about the key. But this . . ." Kenji glanced between the book and Julius. "Just get over here." He waved frantically for Julius, and the older boy rushed to meet him. Piper, however, approached Camilla, who was sitting at the base of the bookshelves, nose deep in a book. Several other tomes surrounded her.

It was dangerous to interrupt any reader—Piper herself had once snapped at Atticus for interrupting her during the final pages of a novel—and Camilla probably had the tenacity of twenty readers combined. Piper proceeded with caution.

"Hey," Camilla said as Piper's shadow fell over the pages, and Piper breathed a sigh of relief. If Camilla had initiated the conversation, Piper couldn't be heckled for interrupting her. "Where have you been all morning?"

"Practicing my affinity. I can become invisible."

Camilla barked out a laugh. "Yeah. Good one."

"I'm not kidding."

Camilla cocked an eyebrow. "So disappear now," she challenged.

"I was just practicing with Julius. I'm kind of drained."

"Right. Well, I'll believe it when I see it."

Piper pointed at the books surrounding Camilla. "Find a key in any of these?"

"Ugh, no." Camilla blew out a long breath. "Kenji and

I searched shelf by shelf all morning—dusting as we went, because: *chores*—and once I found the cookbooks, I gave up."

Piper noticed that the book in Camilla's lap was open to a recipe for chicken marsala. "Did my mom really help you learn to cook the way you do?"

"Yes. She was amazing . . . before you showed up. She said I have a natural talent in the kitchen."

"Natural talent would be not burning some basic dishes. But you're like . . . a *chef*."

"Oh my gosh, do you think so?" Camilla practically glowed. "I want to be a chef so bad. Did you know there are entire schools devoted to cooking and baking?"

"Culinary schools," Piper said with a nod. She'd seen an ad once on TV. "You should go to one. I think you'd be incredible."

Camilla frowned at Piper. "Stop being so nice. It makes me want to be your friend."

"And you don't do friends," Piper muttered.

"No. I don't."

"Why? What are you so afraid of?"

It was quiet for a moment, and then Camilla closed the cookbook with a snap. "This is the longest time I've been anywhere. Twenty-two months. But before Mallory Estate, I was moved at least once a year. Sometimes I was in a home for only a few months before they assigned me a new one. Do you know what happened the first time—how I ended up in the foster system?"

Piper shook her head.

"My parents gave me up. They were hollows and terrified of me. They didn't understand how their six-year-old kept making objects melt and morph."

"Camilla, that's terrible."

"You wouldn't understand," she said dismissively.

"No, I do. My mom gave me up too. I was lucky to still have my dad, but I get what it's like not to be wanted. To feel like you aren't enough."

Camilla regarded Piper for a moment. "Well, I didn't have my dad. I didn't have anybody. And moving again and again . . . That change is easiest if you're not losing a family each time. If it's just you, if you don't count on anybody, it hurts a lot less when you get ripped from one home and thrown into another. *That's* why I don't do friends. Happy?" She glared up at Piper, eyes brimming with tears. One blink and they'd break free.

Piper glanced at the floor, not wanting to see it. Camilla was too tough to cry. She was all fire and grit, with a heart of steel. Nothing seemed like it could hurt her unless she let it.

But families were complicated, as Piper knew all too well. She'd tried so hard not to let her mother's abandonment hurt, to pretend she didn't care, but she did. Worse still was the feeling of helplessness that had drowned her when Atticus's condition deteriorated a few months ago. He had limited time left. Maybe half a year.

When the doctors had given them the news, Piper had wished she'd never known her father at all—that he'd died when she was a baby, or left the way her mother had. If she'd never known him, maybe it wouldn't hurt so much to lose him. She was furious that the world would give her this amazing person—a person she loved and looked up to and trusted with all her secrets—only to pull him away. Aunt Eva had called this Piper's anger phase, a natural step in the grieving process. Many days, Piper felt like she was still in it.

"Doing some light reading?" a voice called out.

Piper twisted. Sophia Peavey stood in the entrance of the library, glass doors propped open behind her. She was wearing a long black dress with a high neck, and with her red hair falling over her shoulders, she looked like a black candle lit aflame.

Camilla shot to her feet. Over at the workstation, Julius straightened and Kenji closed the book he was reading and yanked it behind his back. "No. Not r-really," he stuttered. Camilla held up the cookbook and added, "Just some new dinner recipes to try."

Sophia's eyes narrowed. "Shouldn't you all be seeing to that now?"

Kenji nodded enthusiastically and flipped up the collar of his jacket, vanishing from the room. Piper, Camilla, and Julius made their way briskly to the door, but Sophia didn't move aside.

"I would like a word with Piper," the woman said. "Alone."

The two children shot Piper a nervous glance. "I'll be fine," she reassured them. "I'll meet you in the kitchen."

As they edged past Sophia, the woman's hand shot out, falling on Julius's shoulder. "Tomorrow, no more searching the house and grounds for . . . whatever it is you're searching for. After your morning studies, focus on the garden or I will have to *make* it your focus."

Color drained from Julius's face. "Yes, ma'am," he squeaked out.

Sophia dropped her arm, and Camilla grabbed Julius, towing him into the hall. As they slipped out of view, Piper glanced up at her mother, feeling incredibly small. Incredibly transparent, too. Sophia was looking at her as if she could see straight through her skin. It made the hair on Piper's arms rise. It also made her realize that she had no idea what her mother's affinity was. Maybe Sophia was reading Piper's mind right now. Maybe she knew everything Piper had been trying to keep a secret.

"Come sit by the fireplace," Sophia said, and strode past Piper.

Piper followed as if in a trance. They sank into the chairs before the hearth. Now, with the cushion at her back and the massive armrests surrounding her, Piper felt small *and* trapped.

"I want to help you, Piper," Sophia said. "It would simply

be a waste of energy—teaching you if you're a hollow. You understand, right?"

Piper nodded, even though she didn't believe her for a second.

"Tell me what you've been looking for—you and the others. I've watched you search the grounds all yesterday afternoon, dig through the house. Maybe I know the whereabouts of this missing ... thing."

Oh, you most certainly do, Piper thought, then froze. If her mother could read minds, she'd just admitted they were on the hunt for something.

"You can trust me," Sophia insisted. "I only want what's best for you. For all of you."

Not a mind reader, then. But definitely a liar.

"What happened to Grandma?" Piper asked.

"I told you already. She ..." Sophia paused for a moment, brows dipping. "She had to leave for a little while."

In her mind, Piper heard Teddy's words from the day they met. *Your mom had just told me that Mrs. Mallory would kill me and absorb my affinity so she could get the elixir herself.* What if it was only part of the truth? What if Sophia had killed Melena so that *she* could get the elixir? The thought sent a chill down Piper's spine. Could her mother really do something like that? She was cruel and neglectful, but a murderer ... ?

Piper wanted to ask if her grandmother was dead, or if Sophia had trapped her somewhere, maybe the way she'd

trapped Teddy. But her throat felt tight and all she could manage was "Did you send her away?"

"No, of course not," Sophia said softly. "She had some errands to run. She'll be back soon."

Piper shifted in her seat, unsettled by the sincerity of her mother's voice. She sounded so . . . honest. Maybe her affinity had something to do with lying, like being able to bend the truth.

"I can tell you don't believe me," Sophia said, and a sadness touched her eyes. "What can I say to change that?"

"You can tell me what happened to Teddy."

A stillness passed over Sophia's features. Her lips pursed.

"The other kids told me he disappeared," Piper continued. "When was the last time you saw him?"

For a moment, Sophia was elsewhere, her eyes far away. Likely trying to figure out how to most convincingly lie, Piper reasoned. Piper, of course, already knew that Sophia was behind everything—that she'd told Teddy to hide in the garden, that she'd kept his progress secret from the other kids, that she had hidden the key to the first trial and had no intention of sending anyone in there to help Teddy complete it. Probably not until Piper's grandmother was completely out of the picture.

Sophia didn't know what Piper knew, though. This was Piper's chance to catch her in a lie, to prove everything she believed about her.

Sophia continued to stare ahead, palms resting in her lap, eyes almost lifeless. She looked frozen, like a statue.

"Mom?" Piper waved a hand in front of her mother's face. She didn't even blink. *"Mom?"* Piper touched her arm.

Sophia flinched, and when her eyes locked on Piper, Piper flinched too. She pulled her hand away, scooted back into her seat. Her mother's eyes were hauntingly large now, almost too green. "You've grown so big," Sophia said sadly.

"And you missed it." Piper couldn't keep the edge of anger from her voice.

"Some days, I think I never should have left. I had so much to prove, and . . ." Sophia forced a smile. "I have not been the mother you deserve. Not then, and not now. I should . . ." She paused, pressed her lips together. Her eyes narrowed, and their green coloring seemed to dull. The gold flecks at their edges glinted like fire.

Something creaked, and Piper looked up to see the Persian rubbing its head against the library's door. "Rehashing the past is a waste of time," Sophia said as the Persian slunk nearer. "Leaving was necessary. My work was most important."

"More important than family?" Piper demanded.

"Perhaps one day you will understand. Now tell me: What have you been searching for?"

Tears burned in Piper's eyes. "A way into the garden," she gritted out. "That's all I've been doing—it's what all your

children have been doing—and even that isn't enough. Why can't you pretend to like me? What do I have to do for you to care about me even a little?"

The Persian leaped into Sophia's lap, and she stroked the cat's white fur delicately. "Find a way into the garden and bring me the elixir," she said. "If you can't do that, you're worthless to me."

"Worthless?" Piper was crying now. She hated it, wasting tears on a woman who clearly didn't love her—who'd *never* cared about her—and yet here she was, sobbing.

"Find the elixir. It's a small request."

"If it's such a small request, get it yourself!" Piper yelled.

"I will not waste time conversing with someone so emotional. Now go help the others." Sophia waved a hand dismissively.

Not knowing what else to do, Piper stood and walked in a daze toward the exit. Just before the double doors, Sophia called out to her. "Have you found your affinity yet?"

Piper glanced over her shoulder. "I thought Grandma was the one who helped with affinities."

"Some find their affinity on their own."

Piper's locket warmed against her chest. "I haven't found anything," she answered.

Sophia turned to the Persian, stroking the cat's long white fur. "Like I said, worthless."

Chapter Sixteen

The Magi's Guide to the Origin of Affinities

P iper didn't help with dinner prep. She didn't eat anything either.

She fled straight to her room and cried into her pillow until her eyes were puffy and red. Her mother was even more awful than she'd realized, and the tears came freely, as though she were drawing them from a bottomless well. Despite how endless her grief felt, the tears did, in fact, slow, and Piper was left replaying her conversation with her mother, coming back to one detail time and again.

Assuming her mother wanted the elixir for herself, it didn't make sense that she was still hiding Teddy's current situation from the other children. With Grandma Mallory out of the way, Sophia could have given them the key and

sent them after Teddy to complete the trials, but she'd hidden the key instead. Why?

Piper touched her locket through her shirt. She was missing something. The pieces were all there, but they didn't line up properly.

She wished she could speak with her grandmother and ask her what happened. She was so easy to talk to—she had a way of making Piper feel at ease. Just a few weeks ago, they'd eaten a birthday lunch together to celebrate Piper having turned twelve. Melena had sipped on a cup of tea while Piper devoured a slice of cheesecake topped with Snickers pieces, fudge, and whipped cream.

"That's not cheesecake, dear. It's a monstrosity," Melena teased.

Piper frowned mid-bite and pulled the fork from her mouth, making sure to lick the tines clean. "What?"

"Cheesecake doesn't need novelty candy bars on top of it. It's perfect plain, though I would tolerate a strawberry or cherry glaze."

"Grandma, it's delicious," Piper insisted. "And it's *my* birthday, which means whatever dessert I pick is perfect."

"Touché," she replied with a smile. "So nothing is new, truly? A whole year since I've seen you and you have nothing exciting to report?" Her eyes worked over Piper, as if she thought she might find a secret scrawled across her skin.

Piper considered sharing how Bridget had pulled away this past year. First by not asking how Atticus was doing, then by inviting new friends to sit with them at lunch, then by always being busy with these new friends, until Piper found herself out of the circle altogether, eating lunch alone, and wondering how a friend she'd known since kindergarten could abandon her in a matter of weeks. But Piper's grandma didn't want to be bored with those details.

"Nothing is new. Dad's still sick, Mom's still avoiding me, and school is still . . . school. But at least summer vacation starts in a few weeks."

"Don't you fret about your mother," Melena said. "It's her loss, running away like that. If you ever need to talk to someone about . . . anything, you know where to find me."

"Thanks, Grandma. But I've got Dad to talk to."

"I know you do, dear." She reached across the table and patted the back of Piper's hand. "But I'm here too."

And now, when new and strange things were actually happening, when Piper really did need her grandma, Melena M. Mallory was missing. There wasn't a single adult she could turn to. Her own mother was terrible, and her father and Aunt Eva were currently unreachable—not that either of them would be able to help with quests for elixirs or mastering affinities.

Julius can help, Piper thought. *Julius and Camilla and Kenji.*

If she trained with them tomorrow, perhaps she could get some answers. Teddy—and the garden's second trial—would have to wait.

Later, when the moon shone down on the balcony, Piper woke to a knock on her door.

She pushed herself upright, disoriented. The clock on her nightstand read 10:36 p.m. As she staggered from bed, the knocking sound came again, only not from the main door, as she'd first assumed, but the door she shared with Julius's room.

Piper cracked it open. "What?" she asked, bleary-eyed.

"We're having a meeting," Julius said.

"About what?"

Julius grabbed her wrist and towed her across the threshold. Kenji and Camilla were sitting on Julius's bed with a book spread between them, arguing about something.

"That book Kenji was reading in the library today?" Julius began. "It's an ancient magi text, full of old myths and superstitions, half of which are bogus. I mean, it claims that if you steal a magi's amplifier, they'll be powerless, but that's not true."

"It's not?"

"No. Give me your necklace."

Piper handed it over and Julius made a look like, *Go on, try now.* Piper's hand moved to her chest subconsciously. She

151

faltered a moment, feeling naked without the locket. But when she searched deep inside herself, she could still sense her affinity. Pulling it into the world was like swimming while wearing clothing—clumsy, incredibly difficult—and the fact that she was still recovering from all her practice earlier didn't help. But after several attempts, Julius confirmed that she'd managed to make herself flicker.

"You'd be able to do it fully with enough practice." Julius returned her locket. "It's like I said earlier: the amplifier doesn't give or take away your power. The affinity is always in you. I mean, Teddy and Camilla were tapping into their affinities before they even picked an amplifier. But Kenji's still stuck on the final chapter." He rolled his eyes. "Won't stop theorizing for a second. Is convinced we need to involve the cops."

"Why? What's it say? And why am I the last to know?" Piper looked over the room, catching Camilla's eye.

"'Cause you skirted dinner duties," the other girl said. "No one likes a flake who doesn't pull her weight."

"Honestly, it was just because you're still really new here, and when Kenji started jumping to our rooms to gather us, he naturally woke us first," Julius corrected.

"Aw, come on, Julius. Let me have some fun." Camilla smirked.

"Will someone *please* just tell me what's going on?" Piper demanded.

Kenji stood on the bed, the leather-bound book in question clasped possessively to his chest. "*The Magi's Guide to the Origin of Affinities* claims that . . ." He put a finger to the page and read aloud: "'When a magi kills another of their kind, he or she will assume any and all affinities the deceased party once possessed.'"

Piper shuddered. Teddy had said something just like that when they'd met. He'd claimed that Sophia had told him to hide because Melena wanted to kill him and absorb his time-bending affinity. Piper had thought it was just another one of her mother's lies and tricks, but maybe this book proved otherwise.

"It's not true," Julius argued. "A magi's affinity is unique to *them*. You can't randomly absorb someone else's affinity."

"Not randomly," Kenji said with a raised finger. "By killing them. Also, Mrs. Mallory said that the High Order of Magi is made up of some of the most powerful magi in the world, and that many of them have more than one affinity."

"Sure, but you can't *steal them* through murder," Julius insisted. "We've covered all this in our studies. That's not how affinities work."

"Says the novice who didn't know he had an affinity until coming to Mallory Estate," Kenji grumbled. "We only know what Mrs. Mallory and Mrs. Peavey have taught us. This book could totally be accurate."

"It's ancient," Julius pointed out. "Definitely outdated."

But Kenji wasn't listening. "I've been right about Teddy all along. He's dead! Mrs. Mallory, too! Mrs. Peavey killed them and absorbed their affinities."

"Teddy's not dead," Piper said dismissively.

"You don't know that," Kenji argued.

But Piper did. She'd just seen Teddy that morning. Of course, she couldn't admit it without revealing that she'd found a way into the garden and had been hiding it from everyone.

Kenji went on. "For all we know, Mrs. Peavey can now bend time and . . . what was Mrs. Mallory's affinity again?"

"No clue," Camilla said. "Not for her *or* Mrs. Peavey. They've never told us." She paused, eyes widening. "Maybe because they didn't want to give anyone a reason to try to steal it."

"Exactly!" Kenji exclaimed. "Look, something bad happened to Teddy, I know it, and I'm sick of us not doing anything about it. I even confronted Mrs. Peavey about it yesterday, and she just threatened me with basement duty! And no one's seen or heard from Mrs. Mallory since she left to run errands. Since when does running errands take more than a week?"

"My mom said she was seeing to business. Something about research out of state," Piper said, remembering what Sophia had said that very first night at dinner.

"That must be it," Julius said. "She had some errands to see to before starting her research, and now she's traveling for

work. That's way more likely than Mrs. Peavey killing her."

"It's true," Camilla agreed. "Mrs. Peavey's been acting strange, and she hasn't been the nicest lately, but a straight-up murderer?" She gave Kenji a knowing look. "I don't buy it. She's taken us in. She wants to *adopt* us."

"I still think we should involve the cops," Kenji said. "It's like you guys don't even care that Teddy's gone." He slumped onto the bed and wrapped his arms around the book.

Piper bit her lip. Despite everything, she didn't want to go to the cops. There was no way she'd be able to get the elixir for her father once they were involved. Of course, none of the children would get the adoption they craved if she found the elixir and gave it to her father. As soon as her mother realized the elixir was gone, she'd probably call foster services and offload the kids as quickly as possible. But Piper would make sure her father saw to things. That would be better than having Sophia Peavey as a mother. They'd thank Piper for it in the end.

"Of course we care that Teddy's missing, but, Kenji, we've been through this already," Julius said, dragging a hand through his dark hair. "We can't call the cops because every phone we have access to is dead. We can't go to the neighbors because the closest one is a half mile away, and the Persian would find us before we even hit the end of the estate drive. And we can't e-mail anyone, because the Wi-Fi is protected and no one can crack it."

"Hello? I can teleport," Kenji reminded him.

"Only to places you've been before, locations you can visualize," Camilla pointed out.

"Okay, then I'll teleport to someone who can help—at a courtroom or old foster house."

Julius balked. "And you think they'll believe you? They'll probably just send you back here, where you'll get punished for running away and exposing magi to hollows, and then you're—"

"Stuck with a killer foster parent!" Kenji finished.

"Calm down," Julius said. "Mrs. Peavey isn't a killer. That book's just got you worked up. It was written over three hundred years ago. I'm telling you, it's outdated."

"Then where is Teddy? Huh?" Kenji demanded. "Where's Mrs. Mallory?"

"Them being missing and a book claiming killing a magi gives you their powers does *not* mean Teddy and Mrs. Mallory were killed by Mrs. Peavey," Julius insisted.

"I think I can get us some answers," Piper said before the argument could escalate further.

Camilla raised a brow. "How?"

"By sneaking into my grandmother's office. Maybe she has a calendar or itinerary book and there's a perfectly reasonable explanation for why she's been gone so long. Or maybe there are updated books on magi abilities there and we can forget about *The Magi's Guide to the Origin of Affinities.*"

"Don't be ridiculous," Kenji said. "No one can sneak into Mrs. Mallory's office. The Persian will catch you."

"I can," Piper said. "My affinity is invisibility."

Kenji stared.

"I figured it out the other day. Julius has been helping me."

"Wow!" Kenji said. "Well, go! Right now. What are you waiting for?" The boy waved a hand at the door.

"No way. Piper doesn't try until tomorrow," Julius said.

"Who died and put you in charge?" Camilla grumbled.

"I have always been in charge because I'm the only one who actually bothers to think things through!" Julius whisper-yelled. "If Piper goes now, even invisible, the Persian might hear her. It's too risky."

"I'm also pretty drained," Piper admitted. "I practiced a lot today."

"There you go," Julius said, looking relieved to have more support for his argument. "Piper needs to rest up, recharge. She can train with us tomorrow and this weekend, and when we're making dinner on Monday and there's plenty of noise to cover creaky floorboards, *then* she can go. Sound good?" Julius looked to Piper.

It wasn't that she didn't want to poke around her grandmother's office. After her conversation with her mother in the library, she trusted Sophia Peavey less than ever. If anything, Piper was anxious to see what the office might turn up.

The problem was that when it came down to it, Piper wouldn't have to stay here. She'd find the elixir, her father would get better, and she'd go home. But for everyone else . . . Mallory Estate was their home, and they wanted to stay here—together.

What if the answers she found in her grandmother's office weren't good ones? What if Piper confirmed that Sophia wanted the elixir for herself—that she'd done something terrible to Melena and she didn't care about her foster children at all?

"Well, Piper?" Julius said.

"Will you do it?" Camilla asked.

"Please?" Kenji begged.

Three pairs of eyes looked to Piper, eager, hopeful.

She nodded.

Chapter Seventeen

Rivals Team Up

Piper spent Friday morning in the sitting room on the first floor.

The upholstered chairs were pushed aside, clearing a large space for the children to train. Portraits of the Mallory family hung on the walls, as if they were overseeing the lesson. Piper recognized only her mother and grandmother. There was another woman who bore a striking resemblance to Melena—perhaps Piper's great-grandmother; she'd never met her—but after that, the hairstyles and wardrobes of the subjects turned historic. One portrait showed a man with a curling handlebar mustache and wire-frame glasses who reminded Piper of a field doctor she'd seen in her schoolbooks on the Civil War.

Julius rapped his spyglass against a chair to get their

attention, and Practical Application of Affinities began.

The lesson was composed mainly of mental exercises, where Piper had to envision her affinity amid different stimuli (low lighting, loud stomping, Kenji singing out of tune), followed by summoning sprints, where the children filled and emptied their amplifiers at various intervals to help improve their endurance.

All the while, the sitting room's door was kept tightly shut, the curtains drawn, and Piper spoke no louder than a whisper. (Everyone had agreed that if Piper was to sneak into her grandmother's office soon, it was best that neither the Persian *nor* Sophia know that she could become invisible.)

At the end of class, Piper was exhausted, but with additional practice over the weekend, progress came quickly. By Sunday evening, she could draw out her affinity with relative ease, channeling it through her locket and wrapping it around her body in a matter of seconds. Her endurance, however, was a different story. After dropping her invisibility, she always felt drained and needed to rest for a few hours before she could successfully summon it again. Julius promised this would get easier with practice. "It's like lifting weights," he explained. "Right now, you can do one rep, no problem. As you get stronger, you'll be able to do two, four, *six* reps before you need a break."

When Monday rolled around, Piper woke early and poked her head into the hall. She'd put off visiting Teddy for

too long, and with Magi History lessons keeping the kids and Sophia busy for the morning, this was a perfect opportunity to pay him a visit. Later, if anyone asked where she'd been, she'd say she spent the morning walking every inch of the garden invisible—to see if she could trigger an entrance in that form. She'd have answers tonight after searching her grandmother's office, and she could fill the others in on what was going on then. But for now, secrecy remained the only option. Which meant getting to the garden unseen.

After confirming that the coast was clear, Piper grabbed her backpack and stepped into the hall. The instant she shut her door, she heard the Persian meowing from out of view. Near the stairs, if she had to guess.

She reached into her core and found her affinity with ease. An evening of rest had done her wonders. With a sharp focus, she channeled her affinity into her locket and then around her, vanishing a heartbeat before the Persian slunk into the hall. Its yellow eyes searched the shadows, gleaming.

Holding her breath, Piper took a step forward. The soft blanket of invisibility held. All that formal training in the sitting room was paying off.

She continued on, moving soundlessly down the hall and leaving plenty of space between her and the cat. It looked toward her just once, when a floorboard creaked underfoot, but then resumed its march down the hall. The Persian lay before Piper's room and flicked its tail, watching the door.

Piper shuddered and turned for the stairs, descending them with painstaking care. In the kitchen she rummaged for supplies at a snail's pace. It was growing difficult to keep her invisibility in place as she moved, harder still to extend that invisibility to the items she was picking up and stowing in her backpack.

Finally she was on the patio, the weight of her affinity multiplying. The blanket around her felt like the lead ones the dentist used during X-rays.

Gritting her teeth, Piper climbed the stag and sized up her jump. She wouldn't be able to hold her invisibility much longer. Just thinking about it caused sweat to bead across her brow. Praying no one was peering out the estate windows, Piper jumped. She felt her affinity vanish mid-roll, but by then, the true state of the garden had swallowed her.

She swayed a moment after landing, feeling woozy. She didn't need to reach for her affinity to know she was empty, that it would be several hours before she could even dream of summoning it again. She just hoped she'd be ready when it came time to head to Melena's office.

"Teddy!" Piper yelled, making her way up the oak alley. "Teddy, wake up and get your butt over here with that new key."

Morning sun filtered through the oak branches, dappling the ground with light. When Piper reached the end of the alley, the path forked, and she randomly turned left, still

calling for Teddy as she went. She should really ask him where he slept at night.

The path brought her toward the western fountain of Fates. The long rectangular pool of water rippled from the fountain spray, reflecting light off the statues' golden robes. Piper stared up at the Fate with the shears. The blades looked sharp, perfectly capable of severing a thread of life.

She could still remember the first time she'd experienced death: a coyote had gotten through a loose bit of fencing on her father's chicken coop and enjoyed a midnight feast. Piper had been seven.

Atticus had explained that no animal lives forever—not humans or chickens—and sometimes life has unexpected plans. Death was natural, a critical part of the circle of life.

It didn't matter how patiently he explained everything. Piper was distraught. She insisted that the chickens had escaped into the night and were living in the wild, content and liberated. (Atticus hadn't let her see the chicken coop until after he cleaned it, so for all she knew, this could very well have been the case.) Now, of course, she could see that her father had tried to spare her some of the pain. But if death was inevitable, it meant no one could be spared it forever. That Fate could snip her shears and claim anyone.

Unless, of course, you had the elixir.

"Oh good, you brought food," Teddy said, appearing at the edge of the fountain. "I'm starving." He all but ripped

the backpack from Piper's shoulders and tore into a croissant.

"I'm so sorry! I got caught in lessons on Friday, and then there wasn't a good time to get away on the weekend. I brought you a literal feast to make up for it."

"Nothing like fresh baked goods," Teddy said through a giant mouthful, and continued his assault on the croissant. When he'd devoured it in mere seconds, he immediately started on another, grinning up at her from beneath the brim of his Red Sox cap, his cheeks so full of pastry he looked like a chipmunk. Ugh. Sox fans were heathens.

"So, any updates on Mrs. Mallory or where she disappeared to?"

"Still working on that," Piper said. "I might have some answers tonight."

"I take it this means I'm still stuck in here? That you don't want me coming out until you know where she went?"

"Yeah. I'm sorry, Teddy. I just need you to hang tight for a bit longer."

"Can do, so long as you keep bringing me food." He pulled a granola bar from the bag, and Piper turned her attention back to the Fates.

"Do you think my mother would kill someone to get the elixir?" she asked.

"No. Definitely not."

"Oh, come on. She locked you in here!"

"I'm not *locked in*. If I was really desperate, I could

time-bend back to before the garden was concealed and walk out, then time-bend back home if I needed to. But I've got you bringing me food now."

Piper glanced toward Mallory Estate, derelict and crumbling beyond the borders of the garden. "Who do you think they want to save—my mom and grandma?"

"What do you mean?" Teddy asked with a frown.

"The elixir. Why do they want it so bad?"

"They want it because the High Order of Magi asked them to get it. That's all there is to it."

"And during all those years of searching, they didn't daydream about how it could be used? Plus, my mom made my grandma disappear, and I doubt she did that for no reason. Something doesn't add up."

Teddy looked at her seriously. "Why would anyone want a drink that makes you immortal?" It was a question, but Piper could tell from Teddy's tone that he already knew the answer. When she didn't supply one, he sighed. "Come on, Piper. If you could reverse engineer that drink—if you could make more—you'd be rich. That's what the High Order always feared. It's what Mrs. Peavey and Mrs. Mallory feared too, which is why they're helping the HOM, but something changed. Your grandma's motives, I think. Unless your mom was lying when she told me to hide."

"I *know* that she was lying. My grandma's a good person. My mom is *not*."

"Regardless of what they'd do with the elixir, I know what you'd do. After the fear portal, it's obvious. You'd use it to save your father."

Piper peered at him. "And how do you feel about that?"

Teddy shrugged. "I think it's awesome."

"Oh. I thought you'd want to be adopted like everyone back at the house. I figured you'd fight me when I said I wanted to bring the elixir to my dad."

"Not if the adults are all going dark side, and bringing it to them means it will be replicated and used for all the wrong reasons."

"But what about the High Order of Magi? They're waiting for you guys to find it."

"Piper." Teddy licked the last granola bar crumbs from his fingers and started to peel a banana. "The HOM could conceal it somewhere new and an artifact hunter might *still* track it down a few years from now. The truth is, the elixir is getting out of this garden one way or another. Your mom and grandma have been after it for years. Camilla and Kenji and Julius want to find it so they can get adopted. And I can't lie. A permanent home is all any of us want. But you and I are here, right now, two trials away from having it in our hands. Eventually, *someone* is going to succeed, so I say, if the elixir is going to leave this place, better for it to be used up all in one go, saving someone's life, than risk it being replicated and sold to the highest bidder over and over again."

Piper looked at him. "You really mean that, don't you?"

"Yeah." He nodded. "It would be used for something good. And then the elixir is gone, unable to be abused, just as the High Order intended. Also, I'm ready to get out of this garden, so maybe this is partially selfish. You use up the elixir, I don't have to stay in here, hiding from Mrs. Mallory or Mrs. Peavey or whoever it is you've decided is the bad guy. We both win."

"And I'll make sure my dad sees you guys into good homes, talks to the right authorities about adoption. I promise."

"I know. I thought that went without saying."

Piper smiled. "Thanks, Teddy." It was nice to have everything out in the open with at least one person, to have no secrets between them. Surprising, she thought as she eyed his Red Sox tee, but nice. "You don't have some ulterior motive, do you?"

"No, I swear. But it is kind of shocking—us working together like this. We're supposed to be rivals." He smirked as his gaze drifted to her cap.

"I'm sure there are plenty of Sox and Yankees fans who team up to accomplish . . . things," Piper said uncertainly.

"Like rooting against each other?"

Piper laughed. "This is going to go really well or very, very badly."

"How about we find out?" Teddy held up the small gold key they'd obtained the other day. "We're in the right place, after all."

Piper looked around. "We are?"

"Yep." Teddy pulled off his socks and sneakers and waded into the shallow pool. Piper ditched hers as well and hurried after him, being careful to avoid the worst of the spray from the spouts. Standing before the very first Fate, she could see a small keyhole in the statue's pedestal, just above the waterline. "Here goes nothing," Teddy said, and slid the key home.

Chapter Eighteen

The Fountain of Fates

lmost immediately, the golden statue shifted, sending a flash of light over the water. Piper and Teddy threw their hands up to protect their eyes. There was a colossal crash, and they both leaped backward.

The Fate had tumbled from her pedestal and was gathering her thread from the water. "Darn threads everywhere. Blasted loom. Honestly, it's a miracle I haven't broken an ankle tripping, and—oh." She noticed them and threw her shoulders back. "I suppose you want to know the riddle."

"Is that what happens next—a riddle?" Piper asked.

"I'm talking to you, so yes. Unless you'd rather not hear it."

"No, no. We'd very much like to hear it," Teddy insisted.

"Colossal bother, all this thread," the Fate muttered, climbing back onto her pedestal. She wrung out her golden skirt and tied back her waist-length hair. "Now, how did it go again . . . ? 'Never more . . . Always some . . .' No, no, that's not it. Something about—ah! I've got it. Ready?" With a dramatic sweep of her arm, she recited:

> *"There is always more, but not for some,*
> *Yet still I will pass steadily on.*
> *A curse only for those who have*
> *A limitless quantity in their grasp."*

"Well?" The Fate stared down at them.

"Can we have a minute to think it over?" Piper asked.

"I suppose," she said. "This is literally my only purpose. It's not like I have anywhere to be." She plopped down on the pedestal and began to work at her loom.

"It's money," Teddy whispered. "Mrs. Mallory was always muttering about how her wealth was a curse. How she had all the money in the world and she still couldn't get into the garden."

"Maybe," Piper said. "But there's not *always* more money. There are depressions and stock market crashes, and come on—I'm sure being rich isn't a curse for *every* wealthy person."

"Yeah, maybe." Teddy glanced up at the Fate. "How many guesses do we get?"

"One, naturally," she said, picking at a length of thread.

"What happens if we guess wrong?" Piper asked.

"Then you've lost your chance. I will return to my solid form and won't repeat the riddle until a new elixir seeker turns the key."

Teddy gulped.

"Okay, what else could it be?" Piper said, tugging him nearer. "Maybe it's something more abstract, like . . . fame. You always read about famous actors and musicians being miserable despite their success. And there's always more room for new talent, but not everyone will get a big break."

"But can fame truly be limitless?" Teddy pointed out. "No one stays at the top forever. I mean, look at the Yankees."

"Just because we haven't won a World Series in a while doesn't mean . . ." She caught sight of the face Teddy was giving her and sighed. "Fine, whatever. I see your point." She leaned against the pedestal, deep in thought.

"Excuse me. Young girl? You're pinching my thread!" The Fate tugged at her line, and Piper felt the thread against her back.

"Sorry," she said, stepping away. Then to Teddy: "I can't think with her hovering over us like this. Let's walk."

"Will you stay here?" Teddy asked the Fate.

"Do I look like I'm capable of going someplace?" She held up her hands, once again tangled in her lines.

"We won't be long," Teddy said. "Just need a little time to

think. Wait! That's it." He pulled his pocket watch out and showed Piper the face. "*Time.* There's always more time; it keeps ticking, passing 'steadily on.' But everyone's time is up eventually. And endless time—living forever—would be a curse."

"Would it, though?" Piper asked.

"Think of all those stories that argue against eternal life. Did you ever read *Tuck Everlasting*?"

Piper had. It was her father's favorite book, but she'd never understood why. Winnie Foster could have spent an eternity with a sweet boy who adored her, but instead of drinking from a spring that granted immortality, she gave her drink to a toad.

"Never mind," Teddy said, slipping the pocket watch back into his shorts. "It doesn't matter. The answer is still time."

"Positive?" the Fate asked.

Teddy looked to Piper for confirmation. It *did* make sense, even if she didn't agree that immortality would be a curse. She nodded.

"Yes," Teddy announced. "The answer is time."

The Fate let out an exaggerated sigh. For a split second, Piper feared they'd answered incorrectly. Then the woman said wistfully, "I was hoping you'd deliberate for hours so I could feel the sun awhile longer. Oh well." She stood and resumed her pose atop the pedestal. The wind shifted and she was solid again, golden finish glinting. Except for her threads, which were now silver.

"Where's the key?" Piper asked. "We're supposed to get a new key."

"Not yet." Teddy pulled the small gold key from the base of the first statue and moved on to the middle one. "Three statues. How much you wanna bet we have to solve three riddles?" He turned the key, bringing the second statue to life.

"Let me guess, my sister didn't stump you," the Fate drawled. "Typical." Thread was pooled at her feet, and she worked diligently, wrapping it all into a ball.

"Don't you have a riddle for us too?" Teddy asked.

"So demanding. But yes, fine, fine, here it is." The Fate paused her work and recited:

> *"I can be short or long, full or empty,*
> *But no matter the start, I am always ending."*

"That's it?" Piper asked.

"Look, I didn't make the riddles, I just recite them. If you have a problem, you have to take it up with the original High Order of Magi, and they're currently all dead. I think. My other sister would know." She jerked a thumb over her shoulder, toward the Fate with the shears.

"It's not an issue," Teddy assured her. "We can figure it out." Then to Piper he said, "What has varying lengths but always ends? A movie, a race, hair?"

"Those things can't be full, though, can they?"

"A race could—full of runners."

"But if it was empty, there wouldn't be a race."

"Good point. Maybe it's"—he touched his pocket watch again—"an hourglass. They come in different sizes. They can be full *or* empty, and regardless, they're always working their way toward an end."

Piper frowned. "We already had a riddle about time, and I don't think they'd do it again. Not with something as powerful as the elixir at stake, something that could make someone live for—" Piper clapped a hand over her mouth. That was it. She'd just solved it. "Teddy, all these riddles . . . all the solutions? They're themed around the prize. Every answer somehow relates back to the elixir."

"So the answer is . . . ?" Teddy's face contorted with such confusion that the Fate cracked a smile.

"Life," Piper said to the statue. "A life can be short or long, full or empty, and it is always in the process of ending."

The Fate winked and returned to her original pose, glistening as she became solid. Like with the first statue, the Fate's thread was now silver.

Piper and Teddy hurried on to the third statue and turned the key.

Unlike with her sisters, there was a calmness about the final Fate as she came to life. She regarded each ball of thread she pulled from her pocket with care, stretching a long section of string before she raised her shears. When she

snipped the line, she flinched, as though the cut was a thing she could feel. She noticed Piper and Teddy watching, but did not greet them or ask about her sisters. She simply drew a new ball of thread and recited her riddle slowly, eyes never leaving her task.

> *"A burden, a shackle, a chain, a weight—*
> *You'll cross my path before too late.*
> *And though you may be tempted by vengeance,*
> *I will only be banished through pure acceptance."*

"Death?" Piper said to Teddy.

"That can't be banished," he pointed out. "Postponed, maybe, with medicine or operations, but not banished. Unless you have the elixir . . . But the riddle is phrased in a way that makes it sound like the answer would be true for any person."

"In an everyday situation," Piper agreed. "That's how all the riddles have been."

Together, they ran through everything that fit the theme of life and death and immortality.

Finally Teddy said, "Maybe you're wrong about the theme, Piper. Maybe we should just try to approach it like any old riddle."

She nodded, stumped. They sat at the edge of the pool, toes in the water, ruminating as the Fate's shears snipped and cut.

"Guilt!" Teddy said suddenly. "Everyone feels guilty at one time or another, and it is *totally* a burden."

"You don't banish guilt, though; you have to make amends with what's causing it. At least that's what my aunt Eva would say."

For a woman who ran ad campaigns, her aunt could have had a career as a therapist, Piper thought. She was practically freelancing as one already, always insisting that Piper move past her denial and anger if she ever wanted to make peace with Atticus's diagnosis.

"Grief ends only with acceptance," she was always telling Piper. "And even then it doesn't truly end; you just make peace with what happened, even if it's not fair. It might still hurt, but the grief will no longer be so heavy, so all-encompassing."

Piper glanced up at the statue. It fit the theme, in a way. She didn't believe it—this riddle the Fate presented as law, that a person could move past grief only by accepting it—but it was the only thing that fit.

"Grief," Piper announced, standing.

Teddy looked at her. "Do you want to discuss it first?"

"Trust me, Teddy. The answer is grief."

The Fate smiled weakly. "Unfortunately, yes. Grief can drown a person. You don't beat grief, you learn to live with it. By letting yourself feel it, it becomes a bridge to a new normal." She pocketed her balls of thread and clasped her shears tightly. "Mine is the hardest of the riddles. You've

done well, and I hope this means that you will know how to handle what awaits you."

The statue shifted, and Piper turned away from the reflected brilliance. When she looked back, silver threads dangled from the Fate's pocket, contrasting with her golden robe.

"Where's the next key?" Piper blurted out, but the Fate was solid. "Turn the key again, Teddy. Bring her back to life."

Teddy glanced up from the foot of the pedestal. "It's gone. The key is gone." He moved to the second Fate, the first. "And the keyholes are all sealed over."

"They can't be. We're supposed to get the next key."

"Maybe there's another portal somewhere? Something else we have to do first?" Teddy glanced toward the oak alley.

They jumped from the pool and wrestled on their socks and sneakers—a challenge, given their wet feet. Then they sprinted for the oak alley. It was unchanged.

"I don't understand." Piper fiddled with her locket, pacing beneath the oak leaves. "Solving the riddles was supposed to unlock the next trial. And if we can't animate the Fates again, we're just . . . stuck."

"The Fates!" Teddy exclaimed, and began running back the way they'd come. "That's the problem."

"What are you talking about?" Piper sprinted after him.

When the path forked, Teddy didn't head for the fountain where they'd just solved the riddles, but to the right—toward

the set of Fates on the eastern side of the garden.

"We didn't beat these Fates," he said, panting as they reached the other fountain. "I bet they have more riddles for us." He pulled off his shoes and socks again and waded into the water. Teddy's shoulders slumped as he examined the statues. "Keyholes, but no key." He climbed up the pedestal of the first Fate and waved his arms before her eyes. "Hello? What do we do now? Wake up, you hunk of metal!" He elbowed the statue and then howled in pain, clinging to the gold threads in the Fate's loom to keep from toppling into the water below.

"They're gold," Piper said, staring at the statues.

"Of course they're gold." Teddy scrambled down into the water, cradling his arm. "They've been gold this whole time."

"Not the Fates, their threads. When we solved a riddle and the Fate turned solid again, her thread changed from gold to silver."

"So?" Teddy was now trying to examine the point of his elbow, which had him contorting his arm into odd positions.

"The garden is laid out like a butterfly, right? And butterflies are symmetrical. So if the western fountain of Fates has silver threads and sealed keyholes, then the eastern fountain of Fates—"

"Needs silver threads and sealed keyholes," Teddy finished. "How in the hallows are we supposed to do that?"

"I don't know," Piper admitted. "But we better figure it out."

Chapter Nineteen

Melena's Office

That evening, as the children prepared dinner, Piper wrapped her invisibility around her.

"You sure you can do this?" Julius asked, chopping garlic while Camilla hissed, "I said minced, not chopped. If I wanted giant pieces of garlic, I'd just use whole cloves."

Julius rolled his eyes and looked at Piper. "You're flickering a little."

"I know." Instead of being shrouded in a thick cloak, Piper felt wrapped in cheesecloth. And it wasn't because she was drained. She felt completely rejuvenated after her morning use of her affinity. The truth was that she just couldn't concentrate. She and Teddy had parted ways promising to think about the Fates and how to match the two fountains, and it was taking up all her brainpower.

"Kenji, what are you doing? Use a paring knife," Camilla snapped. Piper watched as Camilla grabbed the steak knife from Kenji and turned it over in her hand. When she passed it back to the boy, the blade was shorter and smooth, a much better fit for the potatoes he was peeling.

"Piper?" Julius said, pulling her attention back to him.

"I've got this," she assured him. "I just have to focus. There's a lot of distraction in here."

"You can do it another night if you need to. No one will judge you."

"Camilla, not judging? Are we even talking about the same person?"

"She'd come around in a few days."

Piper banished the fountain of Fates from her mind and homed in on her amplifier, filling it to the brim. Her affinity strengthened around her, a warm, thick cocoon. "Better?"

Julius peered in her direction. "Better. Be careful, though. Stay focused."

Even though he couldn't see her, she nodded.

The main entrance to Melena's office via the east wing on the first floor was, unsurprisingly, locked.

Piper had to take to the stairs to her bedroom, climb the ivy to the turret, and then take the turret's winding staircase down from there.

The turret's third floor was much like the attic: covered

in dust and filled with storage boxes. But when Piper descended to the second level, everything changed. Here, the turret opened into a sitting area, the room no longer a perfect circle. Only the exterior wall (facing the gardens and the grounds) was rounded.

Beyond a settee, on one of the flat walls, a solid oak door led to what Piper assumed was her grandmother's chambers. And sitting right before the door and meowing sadly was the Persian.

Piper drew a quick breath, nearly losing control of her affinity. The animal glanced her way briefly, then continued to cry at the door. Piper frowned. The Persian always ate dinner with her mother. What on earth was it doing here, in what might be her grandmother's sitting room?

Focusing all her attention on her invisibility, Piper tightened it around herself and descended another flight of the spiral staircase with painstaking care, then entered Melena's office.

The room's perimeter was lined with waist-high bookshelves, an interesting feat given that half the office was circular, like the sitting room above, and nothing could truly be flush against the rounded wall. Books were shelved in every which direction, crammed to maximum capacity. Maps of Blackburn and blueprints of Mallory Estate hung on the wall. In the middle of the room, a mahogany desk was positioned atop a circular area rug, and two chairs were separated by the desk, one for Melena and one for visitors. A

framed picture of Melena accepting some type of award on the steps of the Blackburn Historical Society sat on the desk. Her white hair was piled on her head, and the choker she always wore—black with an emerald gemstone—encircled her throat. Beside the photo was a briefcase, its lid open.

Piper stepped forward for a closer look and something crunched beneath her heel. Startled, she dropped her invisibility. Her eyes went immediately to the spiral staircase, expecting to see the Persian there, but she was alone.

She crouched to the carpet and touched the pebble-like rubble that she'd disturbed. It disintegrated in her hand, leaving a smear of black. Ash.

Piper stood up. There was a ring of it around Melena's chair, as though something had burned there, although nothing in the office appeared damaged. There wasn't even a lingering smell of smoke in the upholstered seat.

Strange, Piper thought, and she tucked the oddity away for later.

Consulting a large calendar hanging on the wall, she found Melena's work schedule at the Blackburn Historical Society. She worked Mondays, Wednesdays, and Fridays from twelve to four, and Tuesdays and Thursdays from nine to four. There wasn't a single note about a research trip—not for this month or last.

Piper turned to the briefcase and sifted through the papers. The first sheet was a blueprint of Mallory Estate's

garden. The butterfly-shaped path was more apparent than ever in this drawn form, and various garden beds were labeled with the flora and fauna they held. The plan was dated 1753.

Beneath it was a letter so brittle that Piper was afraid it might disintegrate if handled roughly. She held it gingerly as she read:

February 13, 1861

Dear Frederick,

I received your letter and am entirely on board with the plans to protect our Order's most valuable possessions. Even now, the newly formed Confederacy does not seem to be yielding, and I fear we are on the brink of civil war. Who knows what the coming months will hold, but one thing is irrefutable: we cannot risk these items being lost, stolen, or destroyed.

I have contacted the others. If they are in agreement, we will all arrive at Blackburn by the end of the month and begin the concealment on your property with the elixir. Thereafter we can all travel together, concealing the other items in turn.

If the HOM ever needs to access the artifacts in the future, a unanimous vote can break the concealment. I also propose we create a back door for each item, so that reaching any item is possible, if only we possess the right affinities.

Your dear friend and faithful member of the High Order,

Clarence Miller III

So the HOM had agreed to hide certain magical artifacts before the start of the Civil War, beginning with the elixir at Mallory Estate. And if Frederick had been living at Mallory Estate, it was possible he was one of Piper's ancestors. A several times great-grandfather or great-uncle or great-something-or-other.

She'd likely have known all this already if her mother let her attend classes. Surely it was covered in Magi History. Maybe Piper could ask Julius for a crash course one evening.

The rest of the items in the briefcase were mainly building and land deeds, which proved that the estate had belonged to Frederick Mallory, most certainly one of Piper's distant relatives given the shared last name. If he'd been among the original members of the High Order of Magi, he'd likely been present when the elixir was concealed in the garden. Teddy might have seen him when he bent time back to that fateful day.

There was also an ancient newspaper clipping profiling the man. Piper scanned the story, surprised to learn that Frederick had left Mallory Estate to his children shortly after the end of the Civil War and moved to Washington, DC, where he went into business with "an old friend, Clarence

Miller." The article didn't explain what type of business, only that Frederick kept it running long after Clarence's death, and even after the death of his own children, some years later. He never returned to Connecticut, except for funerals, and was reported as being in great health when he went suddenly missing from his Washington home in his mid-nineties. A few years later, he was presumed dead.

Piper did a double take at the photograph accompanying the piece—the handlebar mustache, the wire-frame glasses. It was the man from one of the portraits in the sitting room where Julius taught Practical Application of Affinities. He didn't look ninetysomething. More like seventy, tops. The reporter must have used a very old photo.

Beneath all these papers, at the very bottom of the briefcase, was a teal envelope addressed to Melena. A red wax seal imprinted with an elaborate monogramed *HOM* was already broken.

Curious, Piper lifted the envelope and pulled out a single sheet of paper. It was wrinkled, as though it had once been clenched in someone's fist.

Melena M. Mallory,
The High Order of Magi has reviewed your request to break the concealment on the garden at Mallory Estate and extract the elixir of immortality. Artifact hunters do indeed pose a threat to our most valued magi items, and

we understand and appreciate your concern regarding the safety of the elixir hidden on your property.

However, given the fact that it is hidden at a private residence where you are certainly privy to the coming and going of visitors, and because of the manner by which the elixir was concealed (quite thoroughly), and because there have been no developments since your first request to break the concealment several years ago, the HOM has voted against your request 4–1.

We are sorry not to be writing with better news. Surely this is not the response you hoped for. Please rest assured that we considered the matter thoroughly and are convinced that the elixir remains well protected. Should anything change on your premise concerning its safety, please do write to us again.

Sincerely,

Edgar C. Miller

President

High Order of Magi

P.S. Our beloved Agatha is retiring from the HOM at the end of the year, and I know you've long wanted to sit on the Order. I'll put in a good word for you and nominate you when the time comes; the rest is out of my hands.

Piper lowered herself shakily into her grandmother's chair. Everything the kids had told her was wrong. The

HOM wasn't worried about the safety of the elixir. They'd voted against breaking the concealment—Piper checked the postmark—nearly five years ago.

Grandma could have written to the HOM since then, she told herself. *They could have voted differently, started placing kids at Mallory Estate to help.*

But even as she worked through this logic, it felt wrong. Where was the letter confirming the HOM's unanimous vote to break the concealment? Why keep the notice where they rejected Melena's request but not the one confirming that she could remove the elixir?

Melena and Sophia must have moved forward without the HOM's blessing, Piper concluded. Why, she wasn't certain. But they clearly didn't have the unanimous approval of the current High Order of Magi, nor the affinities to access the garden. Which explained why they'd turned to finding magi children, training them in the art of affinities, and encouraging them to discover a way to the elixir.

Piper paused, remembering something she'd read in Frederick Mallory's letter.

Reaching any item is possible, if only we possess the right affinities.

The room seemed to still. Piper's heart beat faster.

She knew how to complete the second trial.

It wasn't that the fountain of Fates was a dead end, it was that Piper and Teddy didn't have the necessary affinities to

finish the trial. But Camilla ... Piper thought of the girl in the kitchen just earlier, turning a steak knife into a paring knife. Her affinity allowed her to manipulate anything inanimate, like a gold thread that needed to become silver.

This was it.

The solution was Camilla.

Piper had to bring Camilla into the garden.

Chapter Twenty

Sophia's Paper

iper returned everything to the briefcase, making sure the documents were in the proper order and positioned as she'd found them. Then she combed over the desk's surface and through the various drawers, looking for a datebook or planner or anything that might explain where her grandmother had gone.

There wasn't one.

But there was a large manila envelope that held a bound document in the desk's bottom drawer. Piper peeked inside, reading off the title page: *Fringe Physics, Metaphysical Anomalies, and the Multiverse: A Scientific Examination of the Possibility of Parallel Dimensions.* It was authored by Sophia Peavey and dated the year that her divorce with Atticus had been finalized, when Piper had been four.

This was the paper that had disgraced her among her colleagues and lost Sophia her family; the end result of years of obsession with Mallory Estate. Piper owed it to herself to read this paper, to understand what had been more pressing to Sophia than her own daughter. If the woman wouldn't give Piper answers, maybe the paper would.

Piper glanced around the room. She'd told the others she'd look for an updated text on magi—to see if affinities could truly be transferred through killing—but there were too many books. It would take hours to sift through all the copies, and she wanted to make it back to the kitchen before dinner ended. She tucked the manila envelope under her arm and pulled her invisibility into place. She could read through her mother's paper tonight, and on a different evening, when she returned the envelope to the office, *then* she could search the bookshelves.

She tiptoed upstairs and past the Persian—still mewling sadly at the door. It was a bit tiring to keep the envelope invisible as well, but soon she was in the attic, dropping her affinity with a gasp of relief. She paused at the window, frowning. Climbing down the ivy to her room would be impossible without two free hands. Piper reluctantly stowed her mother's paper in the desk. She'd have to return for it later.

When Piper made it back to the kitchen, dinner was nearly over. The kids were getting ready to serve the final course, and when Piper peered into the dining room, she discovered that

the Persian was lounging at the base of Sophia's chair. How had it gotten out of the turret? Had it followed Piper somehow?

You didn't search the sitting room very thoroughly, she told herself. *There was probably an open window, a way for the Persian to leap down to the patio. Or maybe there was a cat door, so it can move between rooms.*

Yes, that explained it.

She turned to Camilla, who was working at the counter, a heat gun held over a ramekin. "I need to talk to you."

"Can it wait? I'm kinda in the middle of perfecting this crème brûlée." She moved the torch deliberately, turning the top of the dessert into a golden crisp.

"Sure, how about tonight?" Piper offered.

"Tonight what?" Julius said, passing by them with a stack of dirty dishes.

"Oh, I, uh . . . just wanted to let you know what I found today. In my grandma's office."

Julius glanced toward the sink, where Kenji was washing dishes. "Good idea, updating us first. Wouldn't want to give Kenji any more wild ideas."

"Yeah, exactly," Piper said, forcing a smile.

"Perfect." Camilla straightened from the dessert. After wiping her hands on her apron, she lifted the small ramekin and beamed at it like it was a beloved child. "Well, this needs to be served."

Piper picked up a dish towel and joined Kenji at the sink,

wondering how she was ever going to ditch Julius so she could talk to Camilla alone.

Later, with her backpack in tow, Piper used the ivy to return to the attic. She retrieved the envelope from where she'd stashed it, climbed back to her room, and emptied the envelope onto the bed. The crisp white pages of her mother's report stood out against the navy-blue sheets.

Piper flipped to the first page and began to read. Not that she could understand much. At least half the words went over her head, but there were numerous mentions of quantum mechanics and unstable atoms and dirt samples. Especially the latter. Every other page seemed to have a table about dirt samples. The gist of it, from what Piper could follow, matched what she'd read on the title page: Sophia insisted that parallel dimensions were possible. Or more specifically, that a parallel dimension constrained to a set area could leave behind traces and residue, providing proof that another dimension lurked just out of reach. The entirety of Sophia's research had taken place at Mallory Estate, with all her metaphysical anomaly readings occurring within the walls of the garden.

A note was tucked between the final pages of the paper.

Sophia,
I have read your paper and I am appalled.
How dare you risk exposing us like this! We have had

our differences, but this "scientific research" accomplishes nothing.

Did you expect me to be grateful for this paper, to bow to your genius and tell you how brilliant and loved you are? All you have done is point anyone searching for HOM artifacts to our door. Of course parallel pockets exist. They are the product of the concealment, proof that the magi's items are hidden in an alternate reality. But now, because of your inability to sit quietly, because of your irksome need to be seen as special, any magi hunting for concealed artifacts will know we have one in our backyard. And they will come for it.

You've now lost everything: your respect within the scientific community, your family, and after this stunt, my trust.

You will help me find the elixir before a competitor does, or you can no longer live here.

There was no signature, but it had clearly been written by Piper's grandmother. Melena must never have given it to Sophia, though, because it had been stored with Melena's things—in her desk, in *her* office.

Maybe they'd had the conversation in person. They must have, Piper reasoned, because Sophia had remained at the estate after the publication of the paper. According to Julius, Camilla, and Kenji, she'd spent years helping Melena try

to access the garden. This scientific paper was probably the reason Melena had approached the HOM about breaking the concealment in the first place. The safety of the elixir was at risk. She'd done what was necessary, even when it meant disobeying the HOM's orders.

The pieces slid into place, rearranging in Piper's mind.

Melena still wanted to protect the elixir. It was *Sophia* whose motives must have changed. She no longer wanted to impress her mother, she wanted to *win*. Once Teddy mentioned that he'd found a way into the garden, she'd turned on Melena, getting rid of her so that she, alone, could find the elixir.

A knock sounded on the shared door. "It's us," Julius hissed.

Piper opened the door and Julius and Camilla spilled into her room. "Tell us everything," Camilla said, collapsing on the bed like a beached whale. "Yes," Julius agreed. "What did you find?"

Piper told them about Melena's office—the letter to Frederick from Clarence, how the HOM had agreed to keep the concealment intact, Sophia's scientific paper and the threat Melena had made, as well as her requests to the current High Order of Magi that had both been rejected.

"I don't know why my grandma didn't just let the elixir be," Piper admitted. "She didn't need my mom's help—or yours. The elixir is clearly safe. Artifact hunters didn't come for it, not even after my mom published her paper."

"That's not quite true," Julius said. "There were these two men who showed up sometimes."

Camilla nodded. "They kept asking about the garden. Wanted to tour it. Mrs. Mallory would always turn them away."

"But they kept reappearing—as UPS, lawn services, repairmen, you name it. I think they're hunting for magi artifacts. But they haven't been around since . . ." Julius glanced to Camilla, looking for help.

"About a year," the girl answered. She rolled onto her stomach and propped herself up on her elbows. "I think Mrs. Mallory put some sort of curse on them. Or the estate. I don't know—something to keep them away."

"Or they finally gave up," Julius offered.

"Maybe." Piper grabbed a pillow and squeezed it to her chest. "I guess I just don't understand why my grandma kept pressing things with the HOM. The elixir has been safe all this time. Why wouldn't it stay that way?"

"Maybe she was embarrassed," Julius said. "Frederick Mallory—an original founder of the High Order of Magi— is her ancestor, and the elixir on her property is in jeopardy because her own daughter made a rookie mistake and basically screamed, 'Hey, we have an ancient HOM artifact here!' I mean, what would you do? She was probably trying to address the problem before it got worse. Involve the HOM sooner rather than later."

"Why did Mrs. Peavey even write that paper?" Camilla

asked. "She knows that the elixir was hidden for a reason. She basically betrayed all magi by publishing her research."

"She didn't really . . . get along with my grandma," Piper said, remembering the journal entry she'd read in the attic. "I think she wrote the paper because she wanted my grandma to be proud of her. But then that backfired and eventually . . . I don't know, maybe she just snapped. Decided she was going to find the elixir on her own to prove a point."

"So you think she really is behind Mrs. Mallory's disappearance?" Julius asked with wide eyes.

"Yeah, I do," Piper answered. "It explains the sudden change in her personality, too. How she went from kind to cruel almost overnight, forcing you guys to cook her dinner, not bothering to look for Teddy, letting Julius run Friday classes instead of taking them over herself. Once she got rid of my grandma, she could let the real Sophia Peavey show."

Julius gulped. "Are you sure your grandma's not running errands?"

"There wasn't anything written on her calendar," Piper said. "But there was the strange ring of soot around her chair. Like she'd burst into flames."

"Maybe Mrs. Peavey did that," Camilla suggested. "Maybe she set your grandma on fire."

Julius gulped again. "But . . . why? They were searching for the elixir together for years. Why does she want it for herself all of a sudden?"

"So she can publish a new paper and save her reputation. So she can reproduce the elixir and get rich. Or maybe she always wanted it for herself and she finally decided to act on that." Piper waved a hand. "Take your pick."

"I don't know," Camilla said, shaking her head. "Mrs. Peavey was *so* nice."

"Key word being 'was,'" Piper clarified. "She was nice to me and my dad once too. Then she abandoned us."

Camilla glanced at Julius. "What do you think?"

"I think it's hard to believe, but Mrs. Mallory *has* been missing for a long time—almost as long as Teddy, who Mrs. Peavey doesn't seem that concerned about finding. And now, with everything Piper's discovered...Well, maybe Mrs. Peavey isn't who we thought she was." Julius grabbed one of the posts of Piper's bed. "So what do we do? How do we stop her?"

"About that," Piper said, swallowing. "I think I know. But I need to talk to Camilla."

Julius and Camilla exchanged a glance.

"Alone," Piper added.

"No way." Julius shook his head. "Anything you have to say to her you can say to me, too."

Camilla's cheeks practically swelled with pride. "Yeah, that's right."

Figures she'd take Julius's side now, Piper thought. *She thinks he's a pain 90 percent of the time, but now they're best friends.*

197

Camilla's eyes narrowed. "You're keeping something from us."

"Whatever it is, you can tell us," Julius insisted.

Piper's stomach sank. She had hoped to involve as few people as possible, but the fountain of Fates would remain a dead end without Camilla. The elixir would stay hidden. And the cancer would take her father.

This was the only way.

Piper took a deep breath. "I found a way into the garden."

Chapter Twenty-One

Two Deals

Y ou what?" Camilla screeched.

"When?" Julius asked.

"Shhh," Piper hissed. "The Persian will hear you."

They all looked to the door, waiting, but when the meowing never came, Julius's and Camilla's gazes slid back to Piper. Camilla looked about ready to shoot laser beams at her. "Explain," she demanded.

"I got in last week. Teddy's still in there. I think my mom purposely trapped him." She told them about the invisible entrance above the headless stag, the key Sophia had hidden, how Piper had retrieved it and already worked through a trial and a half with Teddy's help. "Please don't be mad. I didn't want to tell you because I was worried someone would run straight to my mom. I know how badly you guys want to be adopted. And now, after this paper, after everything I found in my grandma's office . . . We can't let my mom have it. Whatever her plan is for the elixir, it's not what the HOM wanted. And if she figures out that Camilla is the key . . . The Fates in the east fountain have to match the Fates in the west. Only Camilla can manipulate the gold to silver."

They both stared at her, unblinking.

"Frederick's letter said, 'Reaching any item is possible, if only we possess the right affinities.' Camilla can complete the second trial. Then we're one step closer to the elixir, and we can figure out how to keep it from my mom." Piper glanced to Camilla. "So can you come in with me tomorrow? Can you fix the statues?"

Camilla slid from the bed, glaring. "You're as bad as Mrs. Peavey—using everyone and caring only about yourself. Like mother, like daughter, I guess. Let's go, Julius."

Julius hesitated only a moment, shaking his head with disappointment. Then he followed Camilla. They left the way they'd arrived, slamming the adjoining door behind them.

The Persian mewled outside Piper's room for the next hour. It had heard the argument, or at the very least, the slamming door.

Piper had no idea what to do next. Without Camilla, she couldn't finish the second trial. And without completing the

second trial, there was no way to the elixir, and without the elixir, she'd never be able to save her father. Her frustration brought her to tears, and she paced back and forth across her room, unable to forget the look of disgust on Camilla's face. Piper could admit that she hadn't been a great friend. But she'd had her reasons for secrecy, and she wasn't *using* Camilla the way her mother was using all of them! That was absolutely ridiculous. Piper wanted to use the elixir for *good*.

Make her see that. Even if you have to tell them everything, including what's going on with your dad.

She smoothed her shirt, took another deep breath, and (after confirming that the Persian had wandered off to spy on someone else) raised her hand to softly rap on the adjoining door.

It swung open a second before her knuckles could fall.

"Don't you knock?" Piper snapped, leaping back.

"Sorry," Julius said curtly. His mouth was thin. Camilla stood behind him with her arms crossed over her chest. "We've been thinking," he said.

"We'll help. Not because we want to help *you*," Camilla said, "but because Teddy needs us. I'm not going to leave him stranded in there because you're a jerk."

"Really?" Piper's heart leaped. She hadn't even needed to tell them about her father. She hadn't needed to say *anything*.

"Yes. A jerk. And a liar. And a selfish, greedy princess," Camilla snapped.

"No, I meant really you'll help? You'll use your affinity to match the Fates?" She was so pleased, she didn't even care that she'd been insulted.

Camilla and Julius looked at each other. Then Julius said, "On one condition. Once we find the elixir, it's ours. Mine and Camilla's and Kenji's and Teddy's. We're getting adopted."

"But my mom—" Piper began.

"Is terrible, apparently. But Mrs. Mallory will honor the promise Mrs. Peavey made us. When she gets home, she'll take us in."

"*If* she gets home," Piper said. "We just agreed earlier that my mom probably did something to get rid of her. And if you bring Teddy out of the garden, my mom will definitely know you've found a way in. How are you going to hide him and the elixir from her?"

"We'll all head into the garden together, and Kenji can jump us to safety," Camilla said. "Then we can head to the historical society, or to the cops. We'll keep searching until we find Mrs. Mallory, and we'll stay a step ahead of Mrs. Peavey the whole time."

"And what if you *don't* find my grandma? You can't run forever."

"Then we'll make sure Mrs. Peavey can never get her hands on the elixir. We'll conceal it for good."

Piper's heart plummeted. "What do you mean?"

"I'll manipulate it into stone, you can turn it invisible, Kenji can teleport it to some obscure place only he knows about."

"I have no idea how to turn an object invisible forever," Piper pointed out.

"What I'm saying is we can hide it," Camilla clarified. "No back doors or keys or trials. That's what you want, right? To keep it safe like the HOM intended?" Camilla narrowed her eyes at Piper. *Unless you're keeping something else from us like I think you are,* the expression seemed to say.

"But that's not *exactly* what the HOM wanted," Piper said. "They left a back door to access all the magi items, just in case. Maybe we shouldn't hide the elixir permanently."

"That's the deal," Camilla insisted. "Take it or leave it."

Piper looked at her friends. Were they even friends? They'd been getting there over the past few days, but now friendship seemed impossible, especially given the way they were glowering at her.

She considered telling them everything right that instant. But what if they didn't agree to give her father the elixir? It would be gone forever if he drank it—concealed from those who might abuse it—and he'd make sure they got adopted. This was the way *everyone* could win, but Piper wasn't convinced that Julius or Camilla would recognize that. They wanted to be adopted so badly, they were unlikely to trust that fate to a stranger. Especially when that stranger was the

father of a girl who'd spent the last week *lying* to them.

So she'd agree to the deal now, and make them understand later. She'd figure out how to get the elixir to her father, and then everything would work out for the best. They'd see.

"Okay," she said, and held out a hand.

"Don't shake unless you mean it," Camilla warned.

Piper kept her hand outstretched. Somewhat reluctantly, suspicion still lingering in Camilla's eyes, the girls shook.

They made plans to update Kenji early the next morning and then head directly into the garden, but Piper couldn't sleep. After reading for a few hours and still not feeling tired, she kicked off her sheets with a grumble and stepped out onto the balcony.

Stars speckled the sky, winking down on the skeletal garden. Tomorrow she'd be one step closer to the elixir. Tomorrow she might even find it.

Her stomach churned. How was she going to break her deal with Julius and Camilla without them hating her? Just thinking about it made her feel sick. She wished she'd been honest from the beginning.

A faraway ringing cut through the house. Piper turned toward her room. There it was again. It almost sounded like a telephone, but according to Julius, there wasn't a single working line at the estate.

She stood rigid as the muted ringing repeated a third

time, a fourth. Then silence spread over Mallory Estate, thick and heavy, until the only thing Piper could hear was her own exhales. Just as she was beginning to think she'd imagined the phone, footsteps sounded in the hall. They drew closer, stopping just outside her room, and someone knocked on Piper's door.

The only person who would be up and confident enough to be out of bed at this hour was her own mother.

Sure enough, when Piper answered the door, she found Sophia Peavey standing in the hall. She was wearing slippers and a silk robe that hung open over a pair of black cotton pajamas. Her hair was pulled into a loose bun and an eye mask had been pushed onto her forehead.

"A call came for you," Sophia said. "From that Eva person."

So the landlines weren't dead after all, at least not in Sophia's room.

"You mean Aunt Eva?" Piper asked.

"I guess. She said you never responded to her text over the weekend, so when the news came, she called me directly. Just to be sure she'd get through."

"What news?" Piper asked. She reached for her locket, terror coiling in her stomach.

"Atticus's health has taken a turn for the worse. She's flying in from Colorado tonight, and she said that Melena or I should take you to the hospital immediately."

The floor seemed to shift beneath Piper. This was it. It

was really happening—the moment she'd been dreading.

"I'll pack my bag," she said numbly.

"I can't take you," Sophia said in a bored tone.

"What? But Aunt Eva—"

"Gave a bunch of orders to the message machine," Sophia finished. "She never actually spoke to *me*. It's the middle of the night; I don't pick up calls at this hour. But I've passed along her message, so that's the end of it." She turned away.

"Wait!" Piper bolted into the hall, blocking her mother's path. "You don't love me, I get that. You never wanted me or hated that I took you away from this estate or whatever dumb reason you have for ignoring me all these years. But I love my dad. And he's dying, Mom. He's *dying*." Sophia wasn't even looking at Piper, so she grabbed her mother's arm. "You have to take me to him."

Sophia flinched from the touch, and her gaze jerked to meet Piper's. The gold flecks in her eyes seemed to wink out, a trick of the dimly lit halls.

"Piper," she murmured, and she looked at her daughter sadly.

"Didn't you ever love *him*, at least? Don't you want to say good-bye?"

"I think . . . It's late, but . . . Yes, I can probably drive you. If I can remember where the keys are." She touched her forehead gingerly, cringing as if from a headache.

"I'll help you search," Piper said.

A meow sounded down the hall, and the Persian slunk into view. Sophia lowered her hand from her brow and stood straighter. "Actually, I have an even better idea." Her eyes glinted brighter now, flashing gold. The corner of her mouth lifted into a smirk. "I'll search for the car keys while you search for the elixir."

"What?" Piper grabbed her mother's arm again, but this time, Sophia merely shook her off. "Mom, he's dying. We have to go to the hospital. Now! I don't know how much longer he has."

Sophia didn't so much as blink. "It's very simple: bring me the elixir and I'll bring you to the hospital. That's the deal." Then she strode for the stairs, the Persian flicking its tail as it followed.

Chapter Twenty-Two

Gold to Silver

This time, it was Piper's turn to burst into someone else's room unannounced. Julius was sleeping—or had been. His grumbles sounded a lot like *Go away* before he rolled over and buried his head beneath the pillow.

"Where's Camilla?" Piper demanded.

"In her room, sleeping, probably. But not me. No, I love being woken up at . . ." Julius checked the clock on his nightstand. "Three in the morning."

"Get dressed," Piper said, grabbing the bedsheets and ripping them back. "We're going into the garden. Now."

Julius grappled for the sheets. "It's the middle of the night."

Piper threw open the closet. "Am I picking your clothes, or do you want to?"

"Okay, okay, I'm up." Julius swung his feet out of the bed. "We're going to get caught, though. You do realize that? There's no way we'll make it through the house, onto the patio, and into the garden without the Persian spotting us."

"We can if I make us all invisible."

Julius's eyes widened. "Can you even do that?"

"I was able to keep an envelope I lifted from my grandma's office invisible. So I think I can do it for you, too."

Julius scrunched up his face. "People are more complex than envelopes."

"I made Teddy invisible with me in the fear portal."

"What the heck is a fear portal?"

"It was the first trial. We had to face our greatest fears."

"So you were scared, and therefore acting on adrenaline, and that is *so* not the same as what you're proposing."

Piper let out a growl of annoyance. There wasn't time for this. "Julius!" she snapped, flinging a hand at the closet. "Get. Dressed. Now!"

"Are you sure this can't wait? Why can't we go in the morning?" He was looking at her the way Camilla had earlier, suspicious and doubtful, and even still, Piper knew she couldn't tell him the truth. If she did, after all this time lying, he'd never help her.

"Because I realized this is our best chance," she said. "Tomorrow is Tuesday. Well, technically today is, since it's after midnight. But the point is now is the best time. If we

wait till morning and skip laundry duty, my mom will know we're up to something. And if we disappear in the afternoon during garden duty, she'll know we got in. But now, at three a.m. . . ."

"She won't have a clue what we've been up to," Julius said, finally following.

"Exactly!" Piper said. "Now please: get dressed!"

Twenty minutes later a very tired, very grumpy group of invisible children stepped onto the patio.

Camilla, much like Julius, was quite upset about being awake in the middle of the night, and Kenji was more confused than annoyed. They'd only been able to give him a quick rundown on what was happening, and while he understood the general plan, he still didn't seem to grasp how Piper had found a way into the garden to begin with. He also didn't seem to care. He was so excited that Teddy was alive and well, and that he'd soon be reunited with his best friend, that he shot from bed and dressed without complaint.

Piper still wasn't sure how she'd ever manage to get the elixir to her father when the three of them intended to teleport off in search of Mrs. Mallory the second they found it, maybe even with Teddy in tow. But she wasn't really in a position to give it much thought. Julius had been right: people were far more complex than envelopes.

Wrapping her invisibility around herself had become

second nature. But to extend it to another being, one with limbs that bent and eyes that blinked and a head that turned and hair that swayed? It was nearly impossible. Piper had been tired when they reached Camilla's room, winded at Kenji's, and straight-out sweating by the time they were on the patio.

She wasn't going to be able to keep this up. Not when they climbed the stag. Her legs felt like jelly. Her breath was coming in gasps. At least in the house, the children had been able to mirror Piper's actions. Moving in step with her. But now they'd have to jump through the garden's entrance one at a time, and Piper felt the weight of her invisibility tripling with each second. She was going to faint if she didn't drop her affinity soon.

"So I just . . . dive forward?" Julius whispered. He was standing atop the headless stag, waggling his fingers at the air ahead. Piper could still see him, just as she could see her own limbs, trembling with exhaustion. In fact, anyone currently under her affinity's blanket could see one another.

Piper nodded to answer Julius's question. It was all she could manage.

"I'm going to break my neck."

"Just go," Camilla hissed, eyeing the sweat on Piper's forehead. "Piper isn't going to last much longer."

Julius nodded and jumped. Even before he disappeared through the portal, Piper knew it wouldn't end well. His

body had been splayed out all wrong. There was no way he'd get his feet back under him properly.

Camilla was next, then Kenji, and when they vanished, the relief was so immense, Piper collapsed to her knees. As she hit the damp stones, she felt the cool evening press in around her. The warmth of her invisibility was gone.

She reached inward, searching for her affinity, but she was empty. Completely used up. So drained she couldn't even sense it.

She'd never experienced this before. Was it gone forever? No: like Julius said, she was a well. Even though she felt bone dry, she just needed time to recharge. Trying not to dwell on the hollow feeling in her core, Piper shoved to her feet, wearily climbed the stag, and jumped through the entrance before her muscles could give out completely.

She landed sloppily, but without twisting an ankle, and then lay back in the grass, panting. Overhead, the stars winked.

"I think I broke my wrist!" Julius was howling. "Don't touch it, Camilla."

"Stop being a baby."

"Can't you see how swollen it is? It's amazing I didn't break the other one after you *landed on me!*"

"Shut up! If you just hold still, I can try to heal the bone."

"I'm a living organism, no thank you."

"But bones are just—"

"Full of live cells and blood and marrow, and thank you for wanting to help but GET THAT AMPLIFIER AWAY FROM ME!"

"Fine, jeez." Camilla pocketed her gold coin. "I'll save it for the fountain."

"Holy hallows," a groggy voice said, and a flashlight cut through the darkness. "Julius? Camilla? What are you doing here?" Teddy staggered up the oak alley. Behind him, the garden was aglow, millions of tiny white lights strung up like Christmas, making every tree trunk and branch twinkle. Piper had forgotten how beautiful it was at night. She'd seen it like this only once—on the evening she'd looked through Julius's spyglass from his balcony and seen the entrance portal above the stag.

"Teddy!" Kenji shouted.

Teddy's eyes bulged. "Kenji!"

The boys sprinted to each other, colliding in a hug that nearly knocked them off their feet.

"You're not dead! You're really not dead!" Kenji exclaimed.

Teddy broke away from his friend. "What's going on?" he asked, passing the flashlight over them. "Why are you all here at . . ." He froze when he saw Piper. "Oh my God. What happened? Do we need to get it for him right now?"

"Everything's fine," Piper said, forcing a smile.

"Get what for who?" Camilla asked, squinting between Piper and Teddy.

"We're here," Piper said to Teddy, "because you guys deserve to be adopted. Camilla will help us beat the second trial, and then we can all face the third trial and get the elixir together. It's your ticket to a permanent home. Kenji's gonna jump you guys—and the elixir—around until you find my grandma."

"She'll honor the adoption promise Mrs. Peavey made us," Julius said. "I'm sure of it."

"But we had to come for the elixir now," Kenji explained, "when Mrs. Peavey and the Persian aren't watching."

Teddy frowned, unconvinced. Was the look on Piper's face *that* obvious? She thought about her father, the smile that didn't reach his eyes. Was that what had happened right now, when she'd forced a smile at Teddy? It was the only thing that could explain why the most trusting person she'd ever met was able to see through her so easily.

"We need to get to the fountain of Fates," she said urgently. "The quicker we do this, the better."

They set off, and Piper could hear audible gasps from Julius, Camilla, and Kenji. They'd never been in this version of the garden—alive and lush—and with the lights making every surface sparkle like crystallized snow, it was extra magical.

"It's something at night, huh?" Teddy said. "Who knew the original members of the HOM moonlighted as Christmas elves?"

Piper shot him a look.

"Right," he said, clearing his throat. "To the fountain."

Teddy brought them to the pool where he and Piper had solved the riddles, and showed Camilla the sealed keyholes and how the Fates' threads had turned from gold to silver. Then the group made their way east, Julius, Camilla, and Kenji taking in every detail of the live garden like wide-eyed children.

Teddy bumped Piper's shoulder as they walked. "What's really going on?" he whispered.

"We just have to get the elixir. Quickly." Piper couldn't say the truth out loud. If she did, she'd break down, and there was no time for that. Every second counted.

"You look . . . like you're not telling me something."

"This from the boy who trusts everyone."

"I just . . ." Teddy bit his lip and searched her eyes. "If something's wrong, you can tell me. You know that, right?"

Piper wasn't sure what did it. Maybe it was the look on his face, pleading and sincere. Maybe it was the fact that she liked how there were no secrets between them, how it made her wonder if this was what it felt like to have a sibling—someone you could count on and confide in. Maybe, above all else, she was just tired of carrying the weight of her grief alone. He'd supported her in the fear portal. He'd support her again now.

She glanced toward the others. They'd pulled ahead

of Piper and Teddy and were thoroughly distracted by the vibrant garden, so Piper whispered an update.

"My aunt Eva called. My dad doesn't have much longer. She said I need to get to the hospital, but my mom refused to drive me—unless I brought her the elixir. So here we are."

"I'm so sorry, Piper." He reached out and squeezed her hand. It was quiet for a moment before he asked, "What about how you promised the others they could use the elixir to get adopted?"

Piper grimaced. "You guys do deserve a home—a real one—but I have to bring the elixir to my dad. He needs it so badly, and I can't risk my mom getting her hands on it." She explained what she'd found in Melena's office and how there was now more proof than ever that Sophia Peavey was after the elixir for all the wrong reasons—and that she'd somehow gotten Melena out of the way to do it. "If I get the elixir, my mom promised she'd take me to the hospital. And then I'll figure out how to give it to my dad and use it up. I won't let her keep it."

"I guess your mom really was the bad guy all this time, huh?" He glanced at his feet, embarrassed.

"Julius and Camilla will be furious at first. But if I give the elixir to my dad, it will be as good as concealed, just as the HOM wanted, and then my dad can see to getting you guys all into good homes. It will all work out. I'll make sure it does. I just hope they'll forgive me in the end. I've lied about so much."

"Don't worry about them. Everything will be great," Teddy said, giving her shoulder a bump. "We're getting that elixir to your dad. I promise."

She glanced at him, heart swelling. "Thanks, Teddy. But I don't even know if that's possible at this point. Julius wants Kenji to teleport us away from Mallory Estate the *second* we have the elixir."

"I'll talk to Kenji while Camilla sees to the Fate statues. Maybe there's a way he can bring—"

"We're here," Julius said from ahead, cutting their conversation short.

They waded into the water of the eastern fountain, and Camilla pulled out her amplifier. She saw to the keyholes first, squeezing her gold coin in her palm as she sealed them shut. Then she moved on to the statues. Piper watched in awe as a metallic sheen worked its way over the Fates' threads, painting the gold silver. Camilla exhaled heavily as she pocketed her coin.

A stillness spread through the garden, so quiet Piper could make out nearby crickets. "The fountains stopped," she realized aloud.

Teddy moved his flashlight over the pool, and sure enough, the spouts spread throughout were inactive. "Check them!" he said.

The group sloshed through the water. "Over here!" Julius called from the first Fate. "It's . . . half a key?" He lifted

something from the top of the spout and held it up for the rest of them to see. It was a dull metal and shaped like a regular house key, only sliced in half lengthwise.

"I know where the other piece will be," Piper said, racing from the fountain and sprinting across the garden. On the same spout, in the western fountain of Fates, was the second half.

Julius handed the first piece over, and like two magnets joining, they sprang together.

Piper held the key between her thumb and forefinger, pulse pounding. This was it, the key to the final trial.

Chapter Twenty-Three

The Infinity Pool

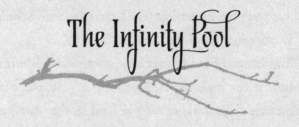

Teddy led the way. The sky was just beginning to lighten when they reached the infinity pool, and the water was the deepest shade of purple-black. Lights from the nearby trees glinted off the surface, making it impossible to see the stairs that curled around the central pedestal and descended into the water.

"So there's just one problem," Teddy said, and pointed his flashlight to where the infinity symbol twisted in the light breeze. The beam of light hit the sculpture's base, where a keyhole waited. "I don't think we can reach it."

He was right. Even with a running jump, the pedestal was too far, an unreachable island in the center of a deadly pool of water.

"What are you talking about?" Camilla kicked off her flip-flops. "Gimme the key. I'll swim to it."

"No!" Piper and Teddy yelled together. They quickly explained why, and Teddy tossed a few blades of grass in to illustrate their point.

"Are you guys forgetting that I can teleport?" Kenji said, clearly offended. "Give me the key. I'll do it."

"You've never been to that exact spot before," Piper said, pointing at the pedestal. "You can see it, sure, but what if you misjudge the distance? If you land in the water, you'll drown."

"Hang on!" Julius expanded his spyglass—awkwardly with his injured wrist—and examined the pool. "There's something here—residue of the work of a magi. Everything's . . . fuzzy."

"Can I look?" Piper asked. "If there was any sort of invisibility spell performed, I have a feeling only I'll be able to see it."

Julius handed her the spyglass. She peered through the eyepiece. And there it was, a small stone bridge that extended from the edge of the pool where they were standing, across the water, and to the pedestal in the center. Piper's amplifier warmed against her chest at the sight of the hidden walkway.

She clacked the spyglass shut and gave it back to Julius. Then she walked forward.

Without his amplifier, she could no longer see the

bridge, but she could practically feel it—a warmth tugging her forward.

"Piper, wait!" Teddy yelled.

But her foot hit something solid, and the others gasped as she moved ahead, seemingly floating in air.

Piper crossed the bridge and scrambled onto the statue's pedestal. Clinging to the rod that supported the twisting infinity symbol, she leaned down and fitted the key into the keyhole. She saw her reflection briefly in the water below, but when she turned the key, the water rippled. There was a thunderous rumble, and for an instant, Piper feared the pedestal was giving way, collapsing into the water, where she would be sucked to the bottom and drown.

Only it wasn't the pedestal that was falling. It was the water. Piper watched the surface level sink down into the pool, lower and lower, until it had completely drained, leaving only a few small puddles on the uneven stone bottom.

Empty, the infinity pool reminded Piper of a well, and at its center, instead of a bucket for drawing out water, was the giant stone column where she stood, a set of stairs wrapping around it and leading into the depths.

Piper looked to her friends. They stood wide-eyed at the pool's perimeter. "Go on," Teddy urged. "What are you waiting for?"

She descended the stairs in a bit of a trance. There was supposed to be a third trial, but the pool had drained

immediately. Maybe the trial was waiting behind the trapdoor. Soon she was in the belly of the pool, bathed in shadow, the wrought-iron handle of the trapdoor in her palm; she was shocked to find it unlocked.

It was almost too easy.

The door heaved open with an ancient creak and a puff of stale air. Piper fanned it from her eyes, and when it cleared, she found herself looking down on a shallow cavity. Inside was a corked glass bottle, round with a slender neck, its liquid a brilliant ruby red. Piper picked it up, fingers trembling. The bulbous part of the bottle fit neatly in her palm.

Here it was. The drink that would save her father.

In the bottom of the cavity, carved into the stone, was a short inscription.

For this magic to work, it must willingly be traded.
Have you truly earned it? Is this fated?

Piper frowned. She'd clearly earned it, because the elixir was in her hands. She'd passed every trial, proven herself a worthy recipient. She'd broken the concealment, and now all that remained was getting the elixir to her father.

She looked up, finding her friends high above, heads craned over the edge of the pool. She lifted the elixir for them to see. Julius beamed. Camilla gave her a thumbs-up. Kenji shook Teddy's shoulder with excitement.

"Bring it up," Julius called. "It's time to teleport outta here!"

But when Piper turned around, a gleaming black portal was materializing at the base of the stairs. Unlike the fear portal she'd entered with Teddy, this portal wasn't pure black. She edged nearer, peering into the darkness. If she stayed still, looking very carefully, she could make out something in the distance. Blurry lights and shapes. There was something long and rectangular and white. A peach smudge above it. Squares beyond the smudge. The shapes pulsed and sharpened, like an image coming into focus.

A pattern appeared on the long white shape.

The squares framed sky.

Piper knew what she was seeing, where this portal would lead. Of *course* it would appear now, bringing her—the finder of the elixir—exactly where she longed to be. She wouldn't need her mother to drive her to Atticus or for Kenji to teleport her to safety. She didn't need anyone.

Distantly, she heard her friends calling for her, but Piper's attention was focused on only one thing: the hospital room, with its stiff bedsheets and sterile windows, and her father lying atop the bed. She could see the heart monitor now. Hear it, even. It was beeping—faint and weak—but there was still time. And at the end of the day, the truth was that Piper didn't care what she'd promised. Now that the elixir was in her hand, she knew she'd break any promise she'd

made to save her father. The way to him had materialized before her. All she had to do was take it.

She glanced up at Teddy. He gave her a quick nod, as if to say, *Do it*, and that was all the encouragement she needed.

Piper squeezed the elixir bottle and stepped through the portal.

Chapter Twenty-Four

The Elixir of Immortality

W hen Piper's father had told her she'd have to spend the summer at Mallory Estate, there'd been only a week left in the school year. The humidity of summer was beginning to creep in, and the air-conditioning was the only good thing about the hospital. Still, she'd have sat in their muggy bungalow all summer without complaint if it meant Atticus could come home.

The cancer, however, had made other plans.

"But I don't want to stay at Mallory Estate," she'd argued when Atticus dropped the news.

"And I don't want to stay at the hospital," he responded, "but here we are. Life doesn't always give us what we want."

That was an understatement.

Her father had looked weaker than she'd ever seen

him, worn away like a pebble in a stream, only instead of becoming smooth, he'd grown jagged. Sharp jaw, hollowed cheeks, bony shoulders and elbows.

"Then let's just go home. Together. We can do the crossword every morning, promise!" It was a desperate offer, because Piper hated the crossword, what with its twisted riddles and wordplay. Was it so difficult just to be straightforward and direct? *I bet doctors love crosswords,* she remembered thinking.

"I would if I could, Pipes. You know that. But I can't. They want to try a final round of chemo, and it will be easiest if I stay at the hospital."

"How often will I see you?" she'd asked, sniffling. "Will Mom bring me? Or Grandma? I want to come every day."

"I don't think that will be possible. But you'll be able to come when I need you. I'll make sure of it."

At the time, Piper hadn't understood what he meant. Now, stepping through the portal, it was clear. Atticus couldn't bear for her to see him like this, withering away. She'd be allowed to come when he needed to say good-bye.

The black walls of the portal dissolved and Piper found herself standing at the foot of her father's hospital bed. His eyelids—paper thin—were closed. The heart monitor crooned in the corner, its tune slow and irregular.

Piper walked forward, still clutching the elixir in her hands. A breakfast tray sat beside the bed. Scrambled eggs

and strawberries and a can of tomato juice with a clear plastic straw poking from it. The meal hadn't been touched. Piper wasn't surprised. Toward the end of the school year, she'd overheard a conversation between the doctor and Aunt Eva when they'd visited Atticus at the hospital. He'd been eating less, losing more weight. There'd been talk of providing more nutrients intravenously, but the cancer was so advanced, the chemo now doing so little, that they decided against it.

Piper uncorked the elixir and a sweet smell wafted from the bottle. She grabbed the straw from the breakfast tray, wiped it clean on a napkin, and dropped it into the drink, then brought the straw to her father's lips. "Dad?" she said, touching his shoulder. "Drink this. Please."

His papery lips found the straw and he sipped daintily. Piper watched the vibrant liquid travel up the straw and disappear into her father's mouth. Eyes still closed, he pulled back and reclined on the pillow, exhausted.

Piper squeezed the bottle in her lap, lips trembling. Did he have to drink all of it, or would a simple sip do? She watched her father, waiting for his eyes to open, for him to sit up, for color to return to his cheeks. Instead his breathing shallowed, the heart monitor continuing to beep at uneven intervals. A doctor burst into the room.

"Is he all right?" Piper asked. "This was supposed to save him."

But it wasn't a doctor at all, just an elderly man wearing

a gray tweed suit. He had a pronounced mustache, and a pair of wire-frame spectacles rested on the end of his long nose. "It will only work if he takes it willingly," he explained.

So *that* was what the inscription beneath the trapdoor had meant.

"And even then, it won't cure him, Piper," the man went on. "It will merely stop him in this moment, freezing the man he is now and preserving it for all eternity. Is that really what you want?"

The stranger stooped down and picked up a briefcase Piper hadn't noticed from the foot of the bed. The name F. MALLORY was engraved in the leather.

When she looked past the wrinkles that mapped his face and the sadness in his eyes, she could see the resemblance to the portrait at Mallory Estate.

Frederick Mallory.

"Consider this carefully, child, because it cannot be undone. To be immortal is to live forever, and forever is a painfully long time indeed. Not even the stars can comprehend it." He smiled kindly at Piper, then slipped from the room.

Piper glanced at the bottle in her hands, then at the heart monitor. Its rhythm was changing, growing more erratic. Atticus Peavey was dying. Her father was dying, and no matter what Frederick Mallory said, Piper couldn't let him die. If he had to willingly accept the elixir for it to work, she'd just have to wake him.

Because he would choose to stay with Piper.

He'd *want* the drink.

"Dad?" Piper touched Atticus's shoulder, shaking him lightly. "Dad, wake up. I brought something for you."

He stirred beneath her touch, groaning.

"Dad?" she tried again.

This time his eyes flickered open, squinting in the hospital light. When he found her sitting on the bed, he frowned. "Piper. What are you doing here?" His voice was dry from lack of use, and the words came out slowly, as though each one drained him even more.

"This will solve everything." She held out the bottled elixir, pointing the straw at him. "Go on. Drink, please. It will let you live forever."

Atticus's thin lips spread into a smile. The smile reached his eyes, and for the first time in ages, Piper was sitting across from the father she knew—vibrant, beaming, bright. Then he opened his mouth and said the last thing she expected to hear: "I don't want it."

Piper shook her head, shocked. "Sure you do. Go ahead. Take a sip." She thrust the bottle toward him.

"No," he said quietly.

"You're not thinking straight. You can't want to leave. You just can't." Piper couldn't keep her voice from cracking.

"Of course I don't want to leave. But I don't want to live forever, either. Then I'd have to watch you die someday." He tilted his head slightly, taking in the sight of her. "Death is part of life, Pipes. We all greet it eventually."

Piper felt her lip tremble. Finding the elixir was supposed to be the hard part, not getting her father to drink it. This was supposed to be easy, this moment right now. This was where Piper was supposed to fix things. "I don't understand," she managed.

"A journey is worth taking because it ends. It has a destination, a finish. Life is the same. I don't want to be stuck in place while everyone moves on around me."

"Dad, if you don't drink it, you're going to die."

"I know," he replied softly. "And I will miss you more than you can imagine. I hate that I have to leave you. I'm sorry about that. It's not fair. But you're strong—you always have been. And I know you'll be okay. I love you, Piper. I love you so very much." Atticus reached forward and squeezed her knee, so softly Piper barely noticed. Then he leaned back against the pillow and closed his eyes.

Piper's eyes stayed fixed on her father as the heart monitor droned on, the beats growing more irregular.

A nurse burst into the room, racing to the bed. Doctors followed. Real doctors this time, not Frederick Mallory.

Piper backed away as if in a trance, the bottled elixir still clutched firmly. Her eyes stayed rooted on her father's feeble form even as the darkness of the portal closed in, swallowing the hospital from view.

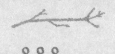

○ ○ ○

When the emptied infinity pool materialized, Piper was beginning to understand her father's decision.

She hated that she did, because the truth was so much harder to accept than believing that the elixir would fix everything. The truth broke Piper's heart.

She wouldn't be saving her father if she convinced him to live forever; she'd be trapping him, just as the apparition of Frederick Mallory had warned.

She had to let him go. To allow him to greet the end of his journey and maybe to start a new one. She'd be okay, just like he'd told her. Not at first. And she'd never be okay with his death. How could she, when a piece of her heart would love and miss him forever? But she would learn to live without him, because that was how it had to be.

The elixir glistened in the bottle, and the contents changed from ruby red to metallic blue. Piper knew, deep down, that the elixir would work now. That before, it was merely dormant.

Have you truly earned it? Is this fated?

Piper had unlocked the ancient magic. She had to be willing *not* to use the elixir to actually obtain it. *This* was the third trial. The elixir would now make anyone who willingly drank it immortal.

Piper looked up. The morning was gray and humid. Storm clouds gathered overhead, but it was still early. There

was still time to say good-bye if she moved quickly. And Kenji . . .

She didn't know how she hadn't considered it before. If the kids were going to teleport to safety, why couldn't Kenji bring them to the hospital—or near it, if he'd never been there before? Maybe this was what Teddy had been about to propose earlier, on their walk to the fountain of Fates. He'd said he'd speak with Kenji while Camilla saw to the keyholes and threads.

She flew up the stairs, two at a time.

"Was that a trial?" Julius yelled. "In that portal-thing?"

"Who cares? It's adoption time!" Camilla cheered.

"Did it work?" Teddy asked, glancing at the bottle still in Piper's hand.

But Piper was barely listening. "The first jump we take has to be to my father in the hospital," she announced after she crossed the invisible bridge.

Julius frowned. "I thought he was traveling for work."

Teddy gave her a look, as if to say, *It's now or never.*

Piper steeled herself and spilled it all. She told them about the cancer and how she'd wanted to get the elixir to Atticus to save him, how all this time she'd intended to use it on him, but how she now understood that the magic would only trap him in a life of suffering. She even explained the deal her mother had made her: the elixir for a ride to the hospital.

"But we won't let her have it," Piper said, cradling the bottle of bright blue liquid. "She'll use it for all the wrong reasons. You guys deserve to get adopted. I just hope that before you go teleporting off to find my grandma, Kenji can jump me to the hospital—or at least to an adult who can *drive* me to the hospital."

"Kenji broke his arm before coming to Mallory Estate," Teddy announced.

The boy nodded. "It was set at Hartford Hospital. I can jump you directly to your father!"

Piper swallowed the lump building in her throat. If she tried to say thanks, she worried she'd burst into tears.

Camilla cocked her head to the side, peering at Piper. "Why didn't you tell us sooner?" Her brow was furrowed, her expression pained. She believed Piper this time, didn't detect even a hint of a lie. Piper's desperation was that obvious.

Piper shrugged. "I didn't think you would let me use the elixir to save him. I knew how badly you wanted to be adopted, so I planned to save him and then ask him to help you guys find permanent homes. Turns out going solo isn't always the best. Sometimes you have to team up with unexpected people." She glanced at Teddy and his Red Sox tee. He beamed.

"I'm glad you came to your senses," Camilla said, "'cause we can't allow any liars on our team. So, no more secrets?"

"None," Piper agreed. "Promise."

Camilla grinned, and just like that, Piper felt it. They were friends now, Piper and this talented girl who kept everyone at a distance.

"Well, what are we waiting for?" Julius asked. "Let's get outta here."

"No way am I strong enough to do more than one of us at a time," Kenji said. "But I'll take Piper first and be right back." He stepped alongside Piper and wrapped an arm around her torso. With his free hand, he flipped the collar of his jacket.

Nothing happened.

Kenji gritted his teeth, furrowed his brow, and flipped the collar again.

Still nothing.

"What's wrong?" Piper asked.

"I don't know. It's like . . ." He stepped away from her and flipped his collar a third time, vanishing from view and reappearing on the other side of the infinity pool. Another flip and he was back beside her. "I think my affinity is only working *within* the garden."

Piper's stomach twisted. "The concealment must keep everything contained. Our affinities work, just within the garden's borders."

"We better get to the patio, then," Julius said. "Through the portal above the stag. Then Kenji can jump us."

"Yes, quickly. Before Mrs. Peavey is up!" Camilla agreed.

Piper nodded and broke into a jog. Soon she wasn't just jogging, but sprinting. Away from the infinity pool, back to the main path. The hospital waited. She had to get there before it was too late.

Her legs pumped faster.

She could hear her friends behind her, following.

The oak alley appeared, and as Piper passed beneath the first few branches, a figure stepped from behind one of the ancient trees.

Piper froze.

It wasn't one figure, but two.

The first tall and elegant.

The other small and white.

Sophia and the Persian.

Chapter Twenty-Five

Mind over Matter

The shock of seeing them made Piper falter. She wanted to disappear, to hide, but her affinity felt like a stone in her stomach. Genuine fear gripped her. "H-how did you get in here?" she stammered. Behind her, Piper could hear her friends approaching. Their racing feet ground to a halt when they spotted Sophia.

"I stood by my bedroom window after we spoke, looking down on the garden," Sophia said. "I wanted to confirm that you'd started your search for the elixir. Imagine my surprise when I saw you appear out of nowhere on the patio. As though you'd been invisible one second, then visible the next. Then I watched you climb one of the stag statues and vanish again." Sophia smiled cunningly. "You may have found your affinity on your own, Piper, but you've yet to master it."

"So you followed me."

"Not at first. I thought you were ambling around the grounds, invisible. But I eventually realized you'd accessed some type of doorway from the stag. And now here I am, so very pleased to see that you've done all the hard work for me." Sophia's golden-green eyes locked on the bottle in Piper's hand. "Now give me the elixir."

Piper pulled it closer to her body.

Sophia let out a small chuckle. "Be sensible, Piper. I'll call you a taxi if you hand it over."

Rage boiled inside Piper. "I don't have time to wait for a taxi. I have to go now, and you know what? My friends understand. They're going to help me, but my own mother won't! How can you be like this?"

Sophia smirked.

"Is it because Grandma made you feel small all your life that you have to do the same to me? Well, you're not her and I'm not you, and he's dying, Mom," Piper said. "The least you could have done was drive me to him so I could say good-bye. We could have said good-bye to him together, but you don't care about anyone but yourself."

Something stalled in Sophia's face, her expression momentarily blank. "You said 'we.' Like a team. Mother and daughter."

"Yeah. I've wanted that forever. I've wanted it since the day you left."

Sophia smiled, but it wasn't the cruel kind Piper had grown used to. This smile was genuine, warm and inviting. Her eyes brightened, turning pure green, and this time, Piper was certain it wasn't a trick of the light. The gold flecks in Sophia's eyes had truly vanished. "Let's go to the hospital," she said, holding a hand out for Piper.

The Persian hissed and Sophia flinched, touching her temple as though she'd experienced a jolt of pain. She jostled her head, straightened, then waved for Piper again. "Come on. Let's go."

Piper didn't have time to explain that she only needed to reach the patio, that Kenji was willing to bring her to the hospital; teleportation would be far quicker than a car ride with Sophia. Nor did she have time to be shocked at her mother's sudden reversal, or wonder if she should trust her at all. Every minute she wasted was less time she had with her father.

But before she could step toward the patio, the Persian hissed again. This time, the noise was unnaturally loud and grating, like a siren's scream instead of a cat's meow. Piper clamped her eyes shut and tried to cover her ears (an interesting feat with the bottled elixir in her hand). When the scream ended, she cracked open an eye. A yellow fog had gathered around the animal, and through it, Piper watched the cat writhe. It splintered and shifted and morphed. The white fur melted away and a dark shape rose from the

ground, sprouting limbs, a torso, a face. Soon a woman stood where the cat had been, a ring of ash encircling her. A bun of white hair was piled atop her head, reminiscent of the Persian's massive tail, and two catlike green eyes blinked at Piper.

"G-grandma?" Piper stuttered.

"Enough!" Melena M. Mallory snarled, batting a hand at Sophia. Piper's mother crumpled to her knees, her skin suddenly pale. "You always were weak, Sophia, but I must say I'm impressed. You nearly overpowered me."

"Shape-shifting," Julius murmured from behind Piper. "One of the rarest affinities."

The ring of ash Piper had found in Melena's office suddenly made sense. Her grandmother had turned herself into a Persian cat, and the ash was a side effect of the transformation, the magi residue left behind. The cat Piper had seen trapped in Melena's sitting room must have been the *real* Wolfe.

"W-where am I?" Sophia gingerly touched her head. Her eyes remained that pure, deep green, no trace of gold.

"Silence." Melena flicked her wrist, and Sophia went quiet. Even when her mouth opened in protest, no sound came out.

"Piper, darling," Melena crooned, one finger on the emerald stone of her choker. "I thought we might reconnect on better terms, but your mother is really failing here, per usual, and well, I've been forced to take matters into my own hands. Now, may I have my elixir?"

Piper remained frozen. She couldn't process what was happening. Her grandmother wasn't missing, she'd been at the estate all along. Disguised as a cat. Spying on her. Following her.

Piper wanted to run suddenly, but she couldn't feel her legs. She reached for her affinity, but it felt forged in steel, almost foreign. It wasn't just that she was tired or drained; something was physically wrong. She didn't feel like herself. A cold fist had tightened at the edges of her mind.

"Mom, do something," Piper pleaded.

But Sophia merely looked up at Piper, shame in her eyes, and the truth slammed into Piper like a sledgehammer: Sophia couldn't fight back, not even if she wanted to. The journal Sophia had kept, admitting that her affinity hadn't presented; her obsession with Mallory Estate and the otherness she'd sensed in the garden; the scientific paper she'd published as an adult because, above all else, she just wanted her mother to love and accept her.

"You're a hollow," Piper whispered.

Sophia nodded slowly.

"Yes, my own blood is a worthless hollow," Melena sneered. "But you . . ." She turned to Piper. "In very rare instances, magi abilities can skip a generation, so I checked up on you every year, at every birthday. You had an aura—I

had a friend check for me—but so did Sophia at your age. I didn't hold my breath. You were proving to be just like your mother—a hollow—but when Atticus proposed we take you in, I saw an opportunity, an angle I hadn't tried. Without proper guidance or the right environment, it was possible your affinity had been suppressed. But Sophia turned on me before I could welcome you to the estate, betrayed my trust and helped Theodore Leblanc escape. I had to improvise before she jeopardized all the progress we'd made." Melena's eyes flicked between Sophia and Piper. "Given how desperately Sophia always wanted my approval, I figured you'd want hers above all else. So I disappeared and left you with dear old mommy, making sure she would drive you toward the elixir every step of the way."

The cruelness, the way Sophia had kept her distance . . . Had it all been orchestrated by Melena?

"You've been controlling her," Piper theorized aloud. "You transformed into the Persian and brainwashed Mom, making her do and say whatever you wanted."

"Two affinities?" Julius muttered, dumbstruck.

Melena smiled thinly. "Yes, the most powerful magi have always had more than one affinity, and after I'd disguised myself as Wolfe, I had Sophia lock the real Wolfe in my sitting room." Her eyes bore into Piper. "And then I had Sophia ridicule and belittle you, Piper. I had her look down on your lack of affinity, knowing it would drive you to try to

uncover one for yourself. After all, every child wants their mother's approval."

"But she tried to fight you," Piper said, thinking about the moments when her mother seemed genuinely concerned about her, different from the dismissive and cold person she usually was. When the Persian had been at a distance and when Piper had touched her mother, Melena's control had momentarily faltered. Piper had seen it in Sophia's eyes—when the golden flecks faded.

But now in the garden, with the Persian right at Sophia's feet, Piper hadn't even needed to touch her mother for Sophia to fight back. Her mere words—a request that they work *together*—had helped clear Sophia's mind and forced Melena to reveal herself.

"She did," Melena agreed, "though she could never keep it up for long. Sophia is always fighting me, unless of course she's trying to impress me. She's been a nuisance since the day she was born." The woman's eyes flicked to Sophia. "I should have taken over your mind far sooner. Maybe then Teddy wouldn't have had the opportunity to mysteriously disappear." Melena looked over Piper's shoulder, searching out the boy.

"Yes, Mother," Sophia said. "All my nuisance research helped me keep Teddy safe. I knew the anomalies created a barrier around the garden, and I knew Teddy would be safe inside the concealment, protected from you until I could reach him."

"He was our only lead into the garden, and you trapped him where he could have starved to death," Melena growled.

"But he didn't starve. And he wasn't truly trapped, either. He could have traveled back in time to before the concealment and stayed hidden in the past. That was all that mattered. Hiding him. Keeping him safe from you."

Melena touched the choker at her neck and glared at Sophia. Piper's mother went pale again, clamping her mouth shut.

"I *knew* Mrs. Peavey didn't want me stuck in here," Teddy exclaimed. "I *knew* she was trying to protect me."

Piper risked a glance in his direction. He still stood behind her, rosy-cheeked from the run from the infinity pool. He'd been right to trust Sophia all this time. She'd truly had his best interests at heart. Piper felt ill at how dismissive she'd been, how she'd laughed at the way he trusted her mother.

"Yes, and by the time I was in Sophia's head," Melena said to Teddy, "it was too late to do anything about your disappearance. I didn't have a time-bending affinity, so there was no way for me to get into the garden. But the key was safe, and I decided to leave it where Sophia had hidden it until another child found a way in." Melena's gaze shifted back to Piper. "I thought you'd run for mommy's praise the second you made any progress. Instead your affinity kept your movements hidden, and your selfish

desire to save your father kept you from confiding in anyone at the estate."

"Selfish?" Piper snapped. "You're the one doing all this because the HOM didn't vote to undo the concealment or make you a member of the Order."

"I do not expect a child to understand the complexities of the High Order of Magi. These concealed artifacts hold some of the greatest magic in the entire world, and they are wasting away. Sophia's paper put the elixir at risk and made our family a laughingstock of the magi community. I am going to reverse that." Melena pushed back her shoulders. "I have a friend with an affinity for duplication. We can produce the elixir of immortality on a massive scale. Sell it to those in need. I will be worshipped. Revered."

"Real noble," Teddy muttered.

Melena squeezed a fist and Teddy choked on his own words. "I am one of the greatest magi alive today. I will not be ignored any longer. Now, Piper, hand over that elixir."

Piper stared, shell-shocked. All these years, her grandmother had stayed in touch not because she cared about Piper; she was merely keeping tabs on a potential asset. That was all Piper had been to her: a thing she could use to achieve her goals.

Her stomach writhed. She felt like she might be sick.

"The elixir," Melena said again, beckoning with a finger.

Why was she even asking? If she claimed to be one of the greatest magi alive, couldn't she just take it?

For this magic to work, it must willingly be traded.
Have you truly earned it? Is this fated?

Piper had earned the elixir by besting the trials, but for that magic to change hands, it had to be willingly traded. A drinker would have to want to live forever to be granted immortality by the elixir. Similarly, if Melena was to be the new owner of the elixir, Piper had to *willingly* hand it over.

A grin spread across her face. She was safe. There was nothing Melena could do. So long as Piper refused to hand over the bottle, Melena would never get the elixir.

That was when she felt the icy touch of her grandmother in her head—that same cold grip she'd felt when trying to summon her affinity earlier.

Piper's grasp loosened on the bottle. She should just hand it over. It *was* selfish, keeping the elixir hidden when the magic could be used to save millions. So much power should be in the hands of an adult. Piper *wanted* to give the elixir to Melena. She *wanted* her grandmother to have it.

She felt her arm moving, extending, holding the bottle out.

"Piper, no!" Teddy shouted.

There was a struggle behind her, and Piper heard Teddy drop to his knees against his will.

Melena was too powerful. If she could control the minds of multiple people at once, Piper didn't stand a chance.

"That's right, Piper," Melena said coolly. "You don't. You stand no chance at all. Just succumb to it. Hand it over."

Something caught Piper's eye—movement among the oaks, something flickering in and out of existence. *Kenji*.

"Don't do it, Piper! Don't listen to her!" Then Kenji flipped the collar of his jacket and vanished.

Chapter Twenty-Six

Forces Unknown

S everal things happened at once, the first being that Kenji appeared directly behind Melena and gave her a firm shove, which caused Melena's hold on Piper's mind to weaken momentarily. Piper shook her head, coming out of a fog.

She pulled the elixir back to her chest, clutching it tightly, only for Melena to lunge directly for it.

She wouldn't have been able to grab it, not if Piper's assumptions about the trapdoor's inscription were correct, but Piper reacted as any sane person would if someone was diving at them. She tossed the elixir past Melena, to her mother, who still sat in the dirt several feet away. Melena growled. Piper scrambled backward.

At the same time, Camilla manipulated the dirt path,

causing it to buck and heave until a series of ruts separated the five of them and Melena from Sophia, who was now crawling for the shelter of the nearest oak tree, bottled elixir in hand.

Kenji jumped behind Melena again, but before he could attack, the woman touched the choker at her neck. Yellow fog swirled as she transformed into a dark falcon. With a flap of its wings, it flew into the storm clouds.

There was a clap of thunder and the sky opened up. Piper was soaked in seconds.

"Everyone okay?" Julius shouted through the rain.

A chorus of yeses sounded through the oaks.

Someone collided with Piper from behind—Teddy. "We have to get you out of here," he said, pulling her to her feet. "Right now."

"I don't have the elixir."

"What?!"

Piper thrust an arm in her mother's direction and Teddy gulped. The barricade of deeply rutted earth stood between them and where Sophia still sat at the base of one of the oaks. Piper yelled for Camilla to flatten the ruts, but a falcon cry overhead drowned out her words. Something swooped through the trees, and Piper felt claws scratch the back of her neck. The locket's chain tightened beneath her chin, then broke. Piper looked up to see the bird—her grandmother—carrying her amplifier away.

A cold voice slid into Piper's head. *Try to hide from me now, Granddaughter.* The falcon opened its claws and the locket glinted as it fell somewhere in the western half of the garden.

"Head for the exit!" Piper shouted. "I'll get the elixir."

A bolt of lightning snaked out of the sky, striking one of the ancient oaks. Fire sparked and embers showered down from the branches.

Kenji yelled, "Camilla, what are you doing?"

Piper swiveled to face her. Camilla's expression was vacant, as though she was in a trance, and she was breaking branches from the oaks and manipulating them into sharpened spears.

"Camilla—no!" Piper yelled, but Camilla had already hurled the spear at Kenji. The boy barely managed to teleport away in time. Julius picked up another spear and flung it after him.

"My grandmother is in their heads!" Piper screamed.

She looked up, searching the teeming rain for Melena. A dark shape flashed between the trees, moving toward the burning oak—toward the very tree where Sophia was huddled with the elixir.

Piper ran.

She heard Teddy begging her to take cover. She saw Kenji zipping around the garden, trying to avoid Melena's control. She glimpsed Camilla fashioning more spears. But Piper ran.

Through the sheets of rain. Across the deeply rutted path.

Toward the burning oak where her mother cowered. Piper had to reach her—had to protect the elixir. Her grandmother couldn't have it.

The falcon dove out of the sky and slammed into the ground in front of Sophia. Fire and smoke billowed. Piper threw up an arm, shielding her eyes. When she lowered it, Melena stood tall and defiant before the burning oak tree.

"I'm so sorry," Sophia muttered from where she cowered on the ground. Her hands were empty. "I couldn't fight her. She was in my head and I gave it up—I passed it to her, willingly."

"It's over," Melena exclaimed. She clutched the glass bottle in her left hand, the blue elixir glinting. Overhead, the oak's branches crackled ominously. The rain was putting the fire out, but slowly.

Piper desperately reached for her invisibility. If she could disappear, maybe she could startle Melena enough to weaken the woman's grip on them. At the very least, she could grab a spear and throw it at her grandmother's head. But while Piper could sense her affinity, she couldn't seem to harness it. She felt porous—like a sponge instead of a well, a pitcher with a fatal crack. She was so drained from earlier, and without her amplifier, she felt . . . broken.

Piper touched the place on her breastbone where the locket usually hung.

"Piper," Sophia managed. She was faint from the heat of

the fire—or maybe from trying to withstand Melena's mind control. Sweat covered her brow. "It's still there. An amplifier is just a tool, but you are the source."

Julius and Teddy had told her the same thing. Yet it was hard to believe in this moment, when she felt small and weak and flawed.

"You are magic, Piper," Sophia said, holding Piper's gaze. Her eyes gleamed, honest and sincere. *"Magic."*

Melena rolled her eyes. "You don't care about her—you didn't before and you certainly don't now." She pointed a finger at Sophia. "Tell her what you said when I told you Atticus wanted us to take her in for the summer."

Sophia shook her head weakly.

"Tell her or I will make you!"

Sophia glanced at Piper, and whatever the words were, Piper knew they would break her heart. The hurt was already plastered across Sophia's features. Piper didn't want to hear it. She just wanted to have this one moment—one small moment—when her mother actually cared.

Melena raised a hand to her choker.

And Piper dove in front of her mother.

She knew she couldn't do anything. Not truly. Her affinity couldn't shield Sophia from Melena's control; it could only make them invisible. But she reached inside and found that her affinity was waiting. She didn't need an amplifier to channel the magic. She *was* the magic.

And she let it fly.

Only this time, it didn't wrap around her. Instead it spilled out, blew away in all directions, rolled like an unstoppable wave. Piper knew, immediately, that this wasn't an affinity she'd summoned before.

The most powerful magi have always had more than one affinity.

Time seemed to slow, and Piper watched her new affinity billow outward at a snail's pace.

Its edges rippled and churned.

It seemed to crackle with energy—with power and destruction.

She sensed, quite keenly, that she might be able to hold this expanding dome of energy in place if she were more skilled with it, protecting anyone inside its borders. Like a force field. But she had no control.

Piper took one final look at the gleaming, life-altering elixir in her grandmother's hand before her affinity met it.

She felt it shatter the glass bottle.

She felt it plow through her grandmother's affinity, aimed now at Sophia.

She felt it crush Melena's grip on Julius's and Camilla's minds.

And when the damage was done, when her affinity had overpowered every bit of magic it had come in contact with, Piper let it disperse like a wave crashing on a beach.

She gasped, breathless, then sank to her knees, completely drained. It would take days before she could draw out her affinity—either of them—again.

For a long moment, the garden was painfully quiet. The thunder had stopped. The rain was a soundless mist. Wisps of smoke rose from the tree, which was no longer on fire.

The children glanced at one another, then slowly turned their attention to the center of the circle.

Melena M. Mallory stared at her bleeding hand, the shards of glass at her feet. Her face went red with rage, and her gaze snapped to Piper. She raised a finger to her choker—a desperate, wild look in her eyes—but instead of retaliating, she stilled. Her finger trembled against the emerald gemstone. Her eyes darted toward Mallory Estate.

Then she transformed into a falcon and fled.

Chapter Twenty-Seven

The Journey's End

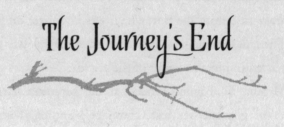

W hat *was* that?" Teddy exclaimed, glancing between Piper and the spot where her grandmother had just been standing.

"Is she gone for good?" Kenji asked. "We should retreat to the house while we can."

Julius and Camilla examined their hands, shocked by what Melena had made them do. Piper wanted to say something reassuring, but Teddy was staring at her. "You can create shock waves," he murmured.

"I think it was actually a force field, like a dome I can hold around me for protection, I just didn't have much control over it."

"Fine, you can create force fields with destructive, shock-wave-like edges," he amended. "That is somehow even *cooler!*"

Piper turned toward her mother. Her hair had fallen from her French twist and hung around her face in stringy sections; dirt covered her hands and knees. She looked almost childlike.

Sophia opened her mouth to say something, but Piper spoke first: "I have to go to the hospital."

"Yes, of course." Sophia shakily pushed herself to her feet and touched her temple. "I remember where the keys are now. Let's go." Piper wondered if her mother could remember everything now that Melena wasn't in control of her mind. Was she aware of all the horrible things she'd said to Piper? How she'd treated Julius, Camilla, and Kenji?

"Thank you, but Kenji said he can jump me there from the patio. It will be faster."

Teddy touched Piper's arm. "I'll help her," he said. "You go ahead with Kenji."

Piper's chest swelled. She hugged Teddy and planted a kiss on his cheek.

"Ugh, what was that for?" he asked, rubbing off the spot her lips had touched.

"Thank you," she said. "Thank you so much." She sprinted for the exit.

Teleporting was sort of like stepping through a portal. Blackness closed in around Piper, and for a moment, all she could sense was Kenji's arms wrapped around her middle.

Then the darkness folded away and she was standing in a hospital room. It was identical to the one she'd reached using the infinity pool's portal.

"I'll go get your mom now." Kenji paused, then asked, "Assuming you want to have her here?"

Piper considered it. "Maybe leave it up to her?" she said finally.

Kenji nodded, and with the flip of his collar, vanished. A moment later he was back, and Sophia Peavey was with him. She'd brushed her hair out of her eyes and wiped the sweat from her brow; she looked more like herself again. The woman smiled meekly and stepped toward the bed.

Piper, however, remained rooted in place. Even after Kenji left, mentioning that he'd be in the waiting room, she couldn't bring herself to approach her father. Instead she watched as Sophia sat on the edge of the bed and squeezed her ex-husband's hand. He stirred and slowly turned his head toward her.

From where Piper was standing, she couldn't see her father's face, but she was reminded of that morning when she was very small and had come to her parents' bedroom. Her mother had been sitting just like this, telling her father that she had to leave. For all the years they'd been apart, for all the hurt between them, the moment was shockingly natural. Perhaps there was no time for grudges or bad blood.

Atticus spoke softly—words Piper couldn't hear—and Sophia responded with something that sounded a lot like, *I'll take good care of her. I promise.*

A nurse bustled into the room. "Oh, good. You're here," she said, noticing Piper and Sophia. "It won't be long now. I was worried you wouldn't make it in time." She checked something on one of the machines, then exited quietly.

Sophia patted Atticus's hand and stood. "I'll give you two some time alone," she said to Piper, and then she followed the nurse into the hall.

The room suddenly seemed very big, the bed very far away. Piper wanted to walk toward it, but she knew the conversation that waited. And what it meant.

Atticus patted the mattress, and Piper made her feet move. The sheets were warm where her mother had sat. Piper threaded her fingers through her father's. They were so bony now, the skin paper thin. "I don't want you to go," she said, tears sliding down her cheeks.

"I know. But we talked about this earlier, remember?"

"What?"

"You had that drink with you." Atticus glanced at Piper's empty hands.

So she *had* been here. The portal had brought her directly to him. She thought it hadn't been real, that it was some sort of illusion. And it must have been, partially. Frederick Mallory had appeared, after all, and he was dead. But

everything she'd said to her father after stepping through the portal, he'd heard.

"Is your journey over, Dad?" she asked quietly.

"Almost, I think." He swallowed, grimaced.

"Will I be able to come there too, wherever you're going?"

"I hope so. But not until . . . you're old. Really . . . old."

There was a long pause. Piper wanted to say a million things. About Grandma Mallory and the estate and her mother. About her new friends and how Atticus couldn't go yet, because he needed to meet them all. She wanted to talk about the bungalow and Carl the penguin and crosswords and aquariums and all the new powers growing inside her. Most of all, she just wanted more time. To talk about everything—especially the meaningless stuff.

"Do you need a copilot?" she asked finally. "On the final stretch?"

"I would like that . . . very much," he said.

Piper lay down and curled up beside her father, as she had after each nightmare as a child.

"I love you, Dad," she said.

"Love you, too, Pipes," he managed.

She stayed there, holding his hand until the very end.

Chapter Twenty-Eight

Another Heart-to-Heart

T hings were different when Piper returned to Mallory Estate, but she didn't notice them. Not at first.

She went straight to her bedroom and cried—for a day, a week, a month. She couldn't be certain. She cried through the funeral. That, she remembered.

It had been a sunny day, which felt right, even if Piper had been a rainfall of tears. Sophia stood by Piper's side, and Aunt Eva kept a hand on Piper's shoulder as the casket was lowered into the ground. Then she was back at Mallory Estate, because Aunt Eva had to see to Atticus's will and then to her clients, and the days blurred together, time continuing to pass even when Piper's world had stopped.

Her friends tried to cheer her up. Camilla brought meals to Piper's room. Teddy sat at the foot of her bed and read her

books from the library. Julius visited with updates on how everyone was doing, and Kenji would teleport into her room to tell her jokes and riddles, desperate to coax out a smile.

Sometimes Piper would scream at them to leave, and they would, and other times she'd sit there and pretend she couldn't see them, but they carried on as though she were treating them well, because that's what friends do: they see you at your worst and keep being your friend anyway.

Aunt Eva even visited a few times, asking Piper if she wanted to come stay with her, leave Mallory Estate behind. But Piper didn't want to leave, especially not her bed. Going anywhere felt like a monumental feat, and all she wanted was to be left alone.

Eventually, ever so slowly, Piper came back to herself. She began to taste the food Camilla cooked, and hear the stories Teddy read, and laugh at the jokes Kenji told.

Julius's updates proved the most surprising.

As it turned out, Frederick Mallory was *alive*. And immortal. Before concealing the elixir in his garden all those years ago, he'd sampled the drink; it took only a small sip for the magic to work.

Then, after watching everyone he loved and admired die by the time he was ninety-four, he'd gone into hiding, content to be forgotten. In many ways, he longed to pass on like his friends. The newspapers had assumed him dead, the magi community as well (which explained the article Piper had

found in her grandmother's briefcase). But when Piper had stepped through the infinity portal, Frederick had sensed it. Using his affinity of incorporeal mirroring, he cast an image of himself to the very same spot, advising Piper as he wished someone had once done for him. Then he projected himself into Mallory Estate and waited for the children. While Kenji teleported Piper and Sophia to the hospital, Frederick explained everything to Julius, Camilla, and Teddy.

"I can't believe you spoke with him in the portal and didn't tell us," Julius said. He frowned. "Actually, I can. A lot was going on." He glanced at Piper's nightstand, to a framed picture of Piper and Atticus sitting on the front steps of the bungalow.

"Frederick promised to get us into proper homes," Julius explained, "but we already have a proper home here. We want to stick together—with Mrs. Peavey. She's back to her old self again."

Julius went on, explaining that Frederick had decided to come out of hiding and serve the Order once more. If he was going to live forever, he might as well do good with all that time. So he'd reemerged in Washington, DC, where the HOM was headquartered, and was currently assisting in their search for Melena. He'd promised to visit Mallory Estate in the flesh sometime soon and was looking forward to speaking with Piper then. In the meantime, Sophia wanted to see Piper. "When you're ready," Julius amended.

○ ○ ○

One day in early August, about six weeks after Atticus's passing, Piper woke feeling different.

How, exactly, she wasn't sure. There was still a gaping hole in her heart. She still missed her father terribly, and suspected she always would, and it felt completely and utterly wrong that he was gone. But she also wanted to leave her room. To walk the estate grounds. To journey. Above all, Piper wanted to see her friends.

So she took a shower, got dressed, and headed for the kitchen. It was at the base of the grand staircase, standing in the estate's massive entry hall, that she first noticed the garden. All those days spent crying in her room and it was waiting just outside her window.

Piper froze, staring through the French doors' glass windows and past the patio furniture, to where the two stag statues marked the entrance of the garden. They were no longer headless. In fact, they looked exactly like the statues Piper had seen *inside* the garden, where everything was alive and flourishing. She rubbed her eyes and looked again.

The heads remained, antlers reaching toward a cheerful sky. Beyond the stags the oak alley towered, green and lush. Flowers blossomed in beds. Grass fluttered in a light breeze. Piper couldn't see it from where she stood, but she knew the pools were now clear of algae and that the crumbling statues were whole once again.

Removing the elixir, unlocking the concealment—it had undone everything. The garden was no longer hidden. Mallory Estate was just an estate. No portals or talking statues or hidden trials. Just a gorgeous home with a beautifully manicured garden.

Piper hurried on to the kitchen, but paused when she spotted her mother in the library. Sophia was sitting in an armchair before the empty fireplace, stroking a ball of white fluff in her lap. Wolfe.

Piper put a palm to the library door and pushed her way inside. Sophia didn't look up, and for a moment it seemed as if she were still under Melena's spell. Then Piper slid into the seat opposite her, and her mother tore her eyes from the empty fireplace, finding Piper.

"I'm sorry. I was having a thought."

"About?" Piper asked.

"Oh, everything," Sophia said, and set Wolfe on the floor. The cat meowed unhappily and rubbed against Sophia's legs before relocating to a plush pillow-bed at her feet. He closed his eyes and purred happily.

"What happens now?" Piper asked.

"I suppose that depends on what you want, Piper." Sophia reached across the space that divided them and took Piper's hand in hers. "Your aunt Eva will gladly take you in. But so would I. Mallory Estate can be your home."

"And I'd live here with you?" Piper said uncertainly.

"Yes, with me."

Piper considered Sophia for a moment, this stranger who was actually her mom. She was still polished and professional—today in a navy-blue pantsuit, her hair pulled into a tight bun—but her eyes looked different. Greener, and more vulnerable, too. The way they had when Melena's spell had broken and the gold flecks disappeared. It changed her entire face. She looked like the woman in Piper's locket again.

Piper reached for her breastbone, her fingers coming up empty.

"You never needed it," her mother said.

"It feels wrong not wearing it, though. Like I forgot to put on underwear or something."

Sophia smiled. "The other children have been combing the garden. I'm sure it will turn up." There was a long pause before she added, "So what do you think?"

"About what?"

"Would you like to stay here, or with your aunt Eva?"

"Julius said everyone else is staying here."

"Yes, for now," Sophia said. "Frederick pulled some strings to arrange it. I'm not sure if I'll ever be able to offer them adoption, but I hope to, and time will tell." She paused a moment. "So?"

Piper bit her lip. Her mother hadn't proposed an option where Piper could go home, but then again, the bungalow would never be the same without her father. It would always

feel empty, like something was missing. Moving in with Aunt Eva meant returning to her old school in the fall; her father and aunt were close and had always lived in the same town. Staying at Mallory Estate meant a new school but not having to say good-bye to the friends she'd made. Mallory Estate also meant more time with her mother, but that possibility didn't bring Piper the joy she thought it might. In a strange, horrible way, staying at Mallory Estate felt like Piper would be replacing one parent with another. A parent who hadn't cared about her for her entire life. It was an insult to Atticus.

"Why'd you leave?" Piper asked sternly, looking her mother in the eye.

"For all the wrong reasons," Sophia said sadly. "My own mother never saw me as worthy, and all I wanted was to impress her. Part of me feared I would never be able to be a decent mother myself until I had. Growing up, I knew about magi and the HOM and hidden artifacts, but because I was a hollow, my mother never told me the truth about the garden. I could sense something odd about it, though, and I thought that if I could prove, scientifically speaking, that Mallory Estate held magic, it would be the next best thing to my having an affinity. It would show her I could at least recognize the work of magi, even if I wasn't a magi myself. But that backfired. I was a hollow who had betrayed her mother's trust, and if anything, she despised me even more after I published my paper."

"Then why didn't you come home—to me and Dad?"

"I'd been gone so long, I didn't know how. So I agreed to help her find the elixir after she told me what was at stake. There were times I considered coming back—when I *wanted* to, even—but something made me stay. Maybe it was your grandma in my head. Maybe I was just a coward. By the time we started fostering, it became obvious she was using me just like she was using the children. I was teaching them, cooking their meals, answering their questions. I was their parent, because the only time she bothered to meet with them was when she was nurturing their affinities or selecting their amplifiers—all to find an artifact that I was starting to suspect the HOM hadn't really told her to extract." Sophia shook her head. "I stayed at the estate because the children here needed me—they needed a mother who cared. But you needed me too, and I want to make up for that now. I would like to be your mother again, if you'll let me. I never stopped being her, really; I was just doing a terrible job at it."

Piper again touched her chest, wishing she could feel the locket beneath her fingers. "Grandma mentioned that you said something when she told you Dad wanted me to stay here for the summer. What was it?"

Sophia swallowed uncomfortably. "You don't want to know."

"Yes, I do. I mean, I didn't want to hear it at the time, back in the garden, but if I'm going to stay here, I think I should hear it now."

Sophia looked at the floor, and it was painfully quiet for a long time. "I said, 'You really think we have to?'"

Piper pulled back, feeling like she'd been slapped. Her mother hadn't been under Melena's control then. How could Piper believe that her mother had truly changed if this was how she'd felt two months earlier?

"Piper, you have to understand how ashamed I was," Sophia said softly. "I've always been a hollow, and my mother made me feel worthless because of it. But I never felt more empty than when I left you and your father. I thought proving myself to your grandmother would make me feel complete—that I'd find what was missing in my life. And when it didn't, I'd been gone so long that shame kept me from coming back. I didn't know how to make it right, so I just . . . decided not to. I hid. I tried to keep you away, knowing how hurt you'd be to learn I was fostering other children. It was cowardly and wrong. I'm so sorry." She squeezed Piper's hand reassuringly. "Your grandmother turned her back on me, and then I made the same mistake with you. I'm glad she brought you here for the summer, even if her motives were wrong; it brought you back into my life, and I don't feel quite so hollow anymore."

Piper nodded, not able to fully understand. How could her mother make the same mistakes *her* mother had? How could she push away someone she was supposed to love?

"I wasted the last decade," Sophia went on. "I never changed my last name back to Mallory, because I always thought of myself as a Peavey—as bound to you and your father. But now he's gone. I missed the chance to make it right with him. I don't want to miss the chance with you."

Piper knew this was where she was supposed to make her choice, but it felt too large of a decision. She wanted Sophia to be the mother she'd always longed for, but she also couldn't trust her fully, not after the last several years.

"I don't know if I forgive you," she said honestly.

"That's fair," Sophia said. "I've done years of harm. But I hope you'll at least let me *try* to make it right. Things are going to change here at Mallory Estate, I promise."

"Can I stay the rest of the summer," Piper proposed, "and see how I feel then?"

"Absolutely." Sophia clapped her hands together. "We can take it one day at a time."

"And can we hang out a little—not just during classes?"

"Come to my room whenever you need me. The second floor is no longer off-limits. I'll plan some fun outings for us too. And I'll do the cooking from now on, and we can eat every meal together."

"Camilla might fight you on that," Piper pointed out. "That girl *loves* her cooking."

"Speaking of Camilla, she was looking for you—she and the others. I think they're out in the garden." Sophia patted the back of Piper's hand, then stood and exited the library.

Chapter Twenty-Nine

The League of Artifact Protectors

Teddy was sitting on the steps between the stag statues. Piper crossed the patio and sat beside him. In the distance, she could hear the rest of the gang playing a game of tag in the garden.

"Hey, you're up," he said in greeting.

"I am," she replied.

"I have something for you." He reached into his pocket and pulled out her amplifier. The locket dangled from the silver chain, winking in the afternoon light. He'd even mended the chain where Melena had snapped it while in her falcon form. "Everyone searched for the first week and then gave up. But not me. I kept at it till I found it. It was hanging from the western Fate's shears. All that time searching the ground and it was dangling at eye level."

Piper threw her arms around Teddy and squeezed him tightly, only letting up when he muttered that he could barely breathe.

"Sorry," she apologized, sitting back and fastening the latch behind her neck. She touched the locket, feeling balanced at long last. It wasn't that she needed the amplifier, but she felt more like herself with it, as if her father were with her.

"You were right about my mom—she *was* on your side," Piper said. "I'm sorry I didn't believe you."

Teddy shrugged. "Hey, from where you were standing, she looked downright evil. I get it."

"But still. I called you overly trusting."

"Which I am. But I appreciate the apology. That's something Yankees fans can't do—admit fault." He peered at her seriously. "Are you sure you're feeling okay?"

Piper laughed, and it felt good. She couldn't remember the last time she'd laughed.

Julius sprinted into view, tearing for the steps with Camilla on his heels.

"I tagged you, Julius Gump," she called. "Quit running. You are out and you've *been* out since the infinity pool."

"Steps are base!" he yelled over his shoulder, and plopped down beside Piper.

Camilla stopped several paces away and hunched over,

hands on her thighs. "Cheater," she said between ragged breaths. "You just made that rule up."

Julius shrugged. "You can join me on base or keep playing, even though you know Kenji will win. He always does."

"True." Camilla climbed one of the stag statues and sat on its back.

"I'm still really sorry I didn't tell you about my dad," Piper blurted out. "That was an awful thing to do to you guys."

"You said all this already." Camilla reclined on the stag's sloping back, turning her face toward the sun. "Quit stressing. You're forgiven."

"And we're really sorry about your dad," Julius said. "The elixir broke and spilled, which is about as permanent a concealment as I can think of, and Mrs. Peavey and Mr. Frederick Mallory are working on our adoption status. Meaning our situation turned out fine. So instead, let's talk about the fact that you have *two* affinities. You have to teach me! I want two!"

"Nothing to teach. Everything I know I learned from the best"—she winked at Julius—"and besides, every affinity you have is already inside you. Right?"

"Unless you killed someone to get that force-field trick," Teddy joked.

Julius gave him a serious look. "Do *not* repeat that around Kenji. He still thinks it's possible that Mrs. Mallory killed someone to get her second affinity."

"Wouldn't that mean he also thinks *I* killed someone?" Piper said.

"He might think that, too," Julius said with a groan.

"So is she really gone—my grandma?" Piper asked.

"No way," Camilla said from the statue. "I mean, the HOM hasn't found her yet, but she's a powerful magi. She's out there somewhere, hiding, biding her time, maybe tracking down other artifacts."

"So what do we do now?" Piper looked between her friends.

"Search for Mrs. Mallory?" Teddy suggested.

"Make sure the other artifacts are safe?" Julius proposed.

"What are we, the League of Artifact Protectors?" Camilla snorted.

"I like that," Piper said with a grin. "It has a nice ring to it."

"I'll tell Kenji!" Julius leaped from the steps and sprinted into the garden, where Kenji was surely waiting to ambush him.

"What about school?" Camilla shouted after him. "Mrs. Peavey isn't going to let us jet around the country after summer ends."

"We'll figure it out later," he yelled back.

Camilla rolled her eyes. "Julius!" He kept running. "Ugh. Of all the ridiculous ideas." She slid from the statue and chased after him.

"She loves him, even if she'll never admit it." Teddy gave Piper a sideways glance. "Should we join them?"

There was no saying where the rest of the summer would take her, or what the months following it would hold. But one thing was certain—Piper Peavey was excited for the journey.

She took off running.

Acknowledgments

First and foremost, I would like to thank my agent, Sara Crowe, who encouraged me to write this story. I'd been sitting on the idea for nearly two decades when I first mentioned it to her. I didn't feel ready to write it and wanted to wait a bit. For what, I'm still not entirely sure, but Sara swore I was ready, that I just needed to start. I am grateful for her gentle nudging. She was right (as she is so often). Once I took the plunge, the story came out willingly, and I'm very glad it is now on paper, in the world, instead of existing solely as an idea in my head. Thanks also to the incredible team at Pippin Properties, for championing this book alongside Sara.

Many thanks are also due to my editor, Krista Vitola, who saw something special in this story, took a chance on it, and knew exactly what I was trying to accomplish with Piper's tale, even if all the right words weren't yet written. Krista's thoughtful queries and suggestions guided me through revisions, and this book is stronger because of her.

To my extended Simon & Schuster BFYR family, for all the hard work they put into this project, with particular thanks to Catherine Laudone, Shivani Annirood, Laurent Linn, and Justin Hernandez, whose gorgeous illustration brought Piper to life so perfectly on the cover.

To the writer friends I rely on for support and inspiration, especially Susan Dennard, Alex Bracken, Jodi Meadows, and Sara Raasch.

To my parents, for planning a trip to Brookgreen Gardens during a vacation when I was a teen, where the elaborate grounds and stunning statues set my creative gears in motion, and to my sister, for being my biggest fan from the very beginning.

To Rob, for believing in me and supporting this dream, even during the hard seasons, and to my children, who make it all worthwhile.

And lastly, many thanks to you, the reader. You are the key that makes this all possible. Holy hallows, I'm grateful.

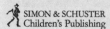